Cantaloupe!

stories

M. Jay Smith

Freehand Books gratefully acknowledges the financial support for its publishing program provided by the Canada Council for the Arts and the Alberta Media Fund, and by the Government of Canada through the Canada Book Fund.

This book is available in print and Global Certified Accessible™ epub formats.

Freehand Books is located in Moh'kinsstis, Calgary, Alberta, within Treaty 7 territory and Métis Nation of Alberta districts 5 and 6, on the traditional territories of the Siksika, the Kainai, and the Piikani, as well as the Iyarhe Nakoda and Tsuut'ina nations.

Library and Archives Canada Cataloguing in Publication
Title: Cantaloupe! : stories / M. Jay Smith.
Names: Smith, M. Jay, author.
Identifiers:
Canadiana (print) 20260218979 | Canadiana (ebook) 20260218995 | ISBN 9781997534273 (softcover) | ISBN 9781997534280 (EPUB) | ISBN 9781997534297 (PDF)
Subjects: LCGFT: Short stories.
Classification: LCC PS8637.M565233 C36 2026 | DDC C813/.6—dc23

Edited by Naomi K. Lewis
Design by Natalie Olsen
Cover image © Pictures Now / Alamy
Author photo by Tim Bulger
Printed and bound in Canada
FIRST PRINTING

FREEHAND BOOKS
freehand-books.com

Canada Council for the Arts / Conseil des Arts du Canada / Alberta Government
CERTIFIED CANADIAN PUBLISHER

FSC www.fsc.org MIX Paper FSC® C100212

!

To Gabi and Milo

What's the difference between a good joke and a bad joke timing!

Contents!

The Two Lolas

1. My hands are of your colour, but I shame to wear a heart so white

Everyone who knew them thought the two Lolas were friends. Why wouldn't they be? They had so much in common. For instance, they lived in the same central neighbourhood, and their kids, Lola Stewart's son and Macbeth's older daughter, were in the same class at the community school. They were the same age, almost exactly, Macbeth being three months younger. They both had brown hair and paler skin, although Lola Stewart sunburnt easily while Lola Macbeth turned a pleasing tan as soon as she went outside. Stewart was medium-tall height while Macbeth was slightly shorter than tall. Both had been born slightly outside of town, further out from the suburbs and bedroom communities and into the real territory of acreages and farms. Both had had biological fathers who had left their mothers alone with children before the children could remember. Each of these men had soon been replaced by stepfathers, although Macbeth's was much richer than the original, while, for Stewart, the new dad's presence was his present.

But the Lolas were not the same. For instance, Lola Macbeth was a star. A professional athlete. A ringette player. She had gone to the world ringette championships four times when she was younger. Ringette, she insisted whenever her prowess came up (she had a lot of prowess to discuss; she was a talented athlete), was a completely different sport than hockey. Back in the height of her career, which wasn't that long ago, she was a media darling. Everyone kind of knew who she was. She was in the papers. Sometimes she was even on television. Normal people would talk about her in hushed tones: I don't know her, but I know *of* her.

Lola Stewart, in contrast, was not a star. By day, she was an assistant at a not-for-profit that supported prisoners and those charged with crimes. The organization provided resources to women in and out of prison and anyone else ensnarled in the criminal justice system. It was not illustrious work. Most days, Lola supported duty counsel, the lawyer who was available to represent those appearing without other legal representation, in criminal docket court. She sat at a small desk by the doors of the courtroom and waited for people to talk to her. Her job was to note names, case information, and whether the person wanted to plead guilty or not guilty. Their third choice was to try to get a lawyer, which would involve asking for an adjournment. Legal Aid was downstairs. They could go see if they qualified that day, if they wanted. (Almost universally, they did not do this. One legal-bureaucratic encounter per day.) So, each day began with a foolscap printout of the individuals appearing that day in court, their names written out beside their respective criminal charges. She drank foul-tasting office coffee in a reusable mug. In the morning, the dingy foyer was bleak and shades of beige: tan upholstered benches with oak accents, off-white walls, sandy carpet. The air held an oil of anticipatory despair. When the courts opened at ten a.m., a flurry began in front of her. It soon coalesced into a long lineup, and for much of the morning she filled pages and ran back and forth to duty counsel's tiny windowless office, no larger than a closet, delivering these notes.

The aroma of alcohol, stale cigarettes, and stress sweat smothered her days. She questioned the logic of drinking before appearing in court. It seemed irrevocably unwise. Yet every day, a haze of booze-stench filled the air. People thought liquid courage. She associated it with hopelessness. One of her friends, whose family background was as similarly without gloss as Lola's, stopped doing this work for reasons like this. It's too depressing, the friend confessed to Lola, seeing these people turn up for court half-drunk, in transparent tank tops, the lace of their neon green bras showing through.

But this aspect of it never bothered Lola. In fact, almost none of it bothered her. That the criminal justice system would be awful to the humans it encountered, by and large, was obvious to her. She loathed the cops and the obscure or ridiculous charges that they pressed against BIPOC citizens. That the minoritized did not know how to interact with the legal system was not a surprise. The egregious dress, the intoxication, the total ignorance about the law. That was all a given. Despair is a product of disempowerment. Bureaucratic incompetence is a symptom of oppression.

Sometimes, however, her hackles rose. This was when wily, dislikable men appeared, intent on disputing the same (inevitable) two types of charges: impaired driving or sexual assault. DUIs made up the bread and butter of many a small crim defence firm, Lola quickly discovered. Most of these individuals were never her clients, because they immediately obtained lawyers, so the lawyers appeared in court instead. The ones who required duty counsel, though, struck her as the foulest humans. Always men, obviously alcohol-coddled, smacking of evil and pickled privilege. She had also reacted almost allergically to a scruffy kid, oozing pervy energy, who announced to her with full confidence that he was there to obtain a publication ban on his sexual assault charges. As if it was something you just requested from a judge who was there to fulfil your desire. Soon after, his parents arrived with the lawyer they, presumably, had hired for him. He didn't need duty counsel, either.

But clients (if you stopped to talk, however briefly, Lola recorded the encounter in a ledger, and the person became a "client" for purposes of the organization's funding) were mostly just more people. There was nothing extraordinary about them. Early on, one of the duty counsel lawyers told her criminal law is seeing normal people in the worst moments of their lives. Lola tended to agree. Sitting at her desk, with the pile of paper naming crimes by their provisions in the Criminal Code, she chose to see it as a privileged vantage.

Docket court was for small crimes, though, so nothing was too dramatic. These were short stories. But they were good stories. Like the sharp-toothed woman with menopausal cheeks and coral lipstick who approached Lola at 10:30 a.m. and had some richly fabricated excuse as to why she wasn't quite on time for her court appearance. She had received the standard notice to show up at ten a.m., because that was when the court went into session, not because that was when she would be heard. Lola knew this, but this woman did not.

The woman's story was obviously, gratuitously untrue, about why she was half an hour late for something that ultimately didn't matter. Also, Lola was no one. Why this elaborate lying about nothing to a nobody? Lola wondered. Because she was then feeling snarky, she looked up this woman's charges and had to stifle a loud, large chortle. She was defending a string of fraud charges.

Or the man in his late fifties, movie-star suave with action-hero sunglasses, who walked up to her and announced that he planned to plead not guilty. (People were always walking up and making all sorts of declarations in front of Lola.) So, you'd like to see duty counsel to enter a plea of not guilty? she reiterated, wanting to pass the correct information on.

Yes, exactly. I'm not guilty of any of it.

She scanned the man's charges. They read like the wireframe for a Hollywood heist film: break and enter, possession of stolen property, disqualified driving, dangerous driving, hit and run, impaired driving, refusal to stop for a peace officer, obstructing a peace officer, resisting arrest. She looked back up at the man, who had been watching her read.

Well, he announced smoothly, his voice glistening cigarette gravel, definitely, some shit went down.

But it turned out he had his own lawyer, milling about somewhere, so he didn't need duty counsel. He casually wandered off. The metric of all of this, Lola observed, the organizing principle, was shame. Who feels it, who can displace it, who can evade it. This guy was doing okay.

Once the initial rush ebbed, Lola went into court and took notes for duty counsel, usually about the timelines the court had proposed for their clients to find a lawyer. Lola loved watching the court. Once, while waiting for opposing counsel to do something or other, the judge and everyone sitting idly, duty counsel brought up an unrelated case, informally. One of his clients had been charged with assault with a concealed weapon, alleging attacking a mall security officer while he was endeavouring to escort her out of the City Centre mall. The Indigenous woman, waiting in the benches, rose to her feet, respectfully, while duty counsel spoke about her. Even though she could have stayed seated, and no one asked her to stand.

This is silly, though, duty counsel said, exasperated. My client swung her jacket over her shoulder as she went to leave! The jacket unintentionally hit the security guard. The concealed weapon? Her cell phone was in her jacket pocket. These charges never should have been brought!

The judge looked contemplative. He rubbed his chin and looked at the woman standing in the benches. But then the other lawyer reappeared and everyone swiftly switched topics. Lola never found out what happened. (She likes to think the Crown dropped the charges.)

And almost every day that she is there, a client whose last name is Cardinal – there are always pages of Cardinals in docket crim court, Cardinal being a common Indigenous last name – appears. Predictably, he comes to ask duty counsel to roll his matter over for another two weeks so that he can obtain counsel from Legal Aid. He arrives with a confession. He's young but looks like he has had a rough time of things. He pleads with her, although she is neither a judge nor even a lawyer, and her job is only to fill out paperwork for duty counsel, to allow him this rollover. He's working on his housing situation, he really is. As the months go by, she assumes that he must recognize her, but she's never sure. He's not beautiful, but he has charm. One week, he comes in to give her an update. Whereas normally he is polite and respectful, today he is drunk and all over the place. He has a job, he tells Lola in a clumsy voice. He has almost sorted out his living situation. He's getting so close. Or, he self-corrects, he has started working for himself, but that counts as a job.

What's the job, then? Lola asks, genuinely curious. Even in this new, drunk iteration, she doesn't find him unlikable.

A rickshaw. I've started a rickshaw company. Actually, he pauses for a beat, it's not quite a rickshaw. More like a couch on wheels.

With that, he goes off to wait for duty counsel, slumping over on one of the benches meant for waiting. Lola Stewart, mulling over what this rickshaw must look like and whether a couch on wheels could possibly be dragged faster than a walking pace, looks up his charges. She flips through the pages of unrelated Cardinals and finds him. His is failure to appear. He's been coming to court biweekly, thinking that he has to sort out all that is wrong with him – a good part of his life is obviously structured around these visits – and it's because he somehow forgot to show up for some probably mostly bullshit charge (or at the very least, almost inevitably minor charge) in the first place. And, really, all he has to do is go down one flight of stairs to the Legal Aid offices and prove to them that he's poor enough that he can be given a state-sponsored lawyer. He is poor enough. Even with the income from his rickshaw-couch company, he's poor enough.

But today he's drunk and tries to pick a fight with one of the security guards. This is not a great idea, Lola knows, though she has never seen this transpire before. A real crim lawyer, his suit crisp and navy blue, intervenes, however. He agrees to ask the judge for an adjournment even though this is not his job, representing random people he finds at the courthouse for free. (Sober up and then go get your Legal Aid application in, he says, world-wearily; a drunk Indigenous kid is nothing he hasn't seen before.)

2. Before my body, I throw my warlike shield

Street hockey was not how the two Lolas met, but it was how they learned to hate each other. Lola Macbeth had only started playing street hockey after she had kids. It was a fun thing to do with friends, she said. She had never even tried it before. If you caught her on a humble day, she'd admit ringette did have some crossover relevancy. But generally, she portrayed her knack for upper-corner goals as being entirely sui generis. Even the men tended to be impressed. Her social media profiles still had her on the podium of one of the times she went to worlds, a gold medal around her neck. Her bios still said she was a pro. For Lola Macbeth, "pro" was an immutable state of being.

Now she was a stay-at-home mom. Her husband, a former triple-A player himself (hockey, that is), was a real estate developer. (He preferred to play in the real beer leagues and thus offered to watch the kids on Sundays.) As a result, there wasn't much pressure for her to go find a job. A different woman might have contemplated a second career, if her athletic zenith had ended, as Macbeth's did, during pregnancy. Growing her second daughter made Macbeth's hormones go haywire. The woman's physique, always substantial, always tough, swelled with improbable weight. It turns out she had destroyed her thyroid.

One day, before her hatred for the Other Lola solidified, she confessed to her at an after-school pickup, some seventy-five pounds into this second pregnancy, breathing uncomfortably, that the weight was totally uncontrollable. In the middle of the night, she'd awake in a wild fervour for food. Shaking and irrational, she could only calm herself by sitting at the kitchen table and eating everything she could find. Thousands of calories later, she could breathe again. Her body was not her own. Not just in the temporary pregnancy way, she suggested, but axiomatically. The weight gain was another foreign body in her body, oppressive and with its own heavy volition.

Once the baby came, Lola Macbeth emerged as a ruin. Her career was obviously over. You could not imagine the two bodies that she had belonging to the same person. With her thyroid destroyed, she'd be on synthetic hormones for the rest of her life. Too much exercise could put her over the edge and trigger her heart. She tried pushing it, of course she did, but her heart accelerated terrifyingly even just walking around the block. Now, her fingers were too fat for her diamond-ridiculous wedding ring. She wore it on a chain around her neck. Women's bodies are meant to expand and contract, slacken and droop. But what happened to Macbeth was a different register of wrong, Lola Stewart thought. It was a more mythological type of metamorphosis. The sort that was reserved, mythically, as retribution for unforgivable sins. Hubris. Avarice. Wrath.

Whereas she was intimidating beforehand, lithe with skill and fitness, the wreck of Lola Macbeth was even scarier. She was larger, certainly less nimble, out of practice, but now she was fuelled with a separate rage. Her blue eyes shone with it. On the tarmac where they set up their street hockey nets, she slapped and checked and shot and used her heft. It was a movement in her hips. And she now reserved, it seemed, the most particular disrelish for Lola Stewart.

3. Ourself will mingle with society

The weekly street hockey had been Jason's idea. A bearded stay-at-home dad in his early forties, Jason, too, had played triple-A when he was younger. He had quit halfway through his first year when he realized he was, fundamentally, a pacifist. There was a ceiling to the game that those who were not bloodthirsty couldn't penetrate. Nowadays, this gave him street cred, but it also meant he despised the competitive spiral of impromptu hockey. He supplied the nets and loaned out sticks and offered his backyard for periodic after-game carousing. Rather than bothering with rules, he curated the players. The game wasn't about hockey, for him, but about *punk*. Punk as a philosophy, punk as a way of life, punk as the zen of punk.

His wife, a doctor, a pediatric oncologist in fact, was less punk, and it wasn't for Jason's total lack of economic pressures that everyone called him a trophy spouse. He was also a babe. His eyes were wide and green, and he had curly, mad-scientist hair that was now half-whitened and creeping back in a perfect widow's peak. His humour was wickedly self-deprecating. After he quit hockey, many years ago, he had started a ska band, which had met with moderate success. (You'd recognize their name if you listened to Top-40 radio back then.) He played the trumpet and sang lead vocals. The band was touring through town when Jason met his wife-to-be: She went to one of his shows, became a groupie, then became his girlfriend. Throughout her medical school, he was the catch, the shiny musician whose band's songs were played on the radio. Then the babies started coming, the band had a creative slump, her career accelerated onto the monied and overworked trajectory that everyone knew it would, and suddenly it didn't make sense for him to do music anymore.

He wasn't quite unhappy. But it was obvious to him that his wife had found him more desirable when he was a mid-level name in Canadian music. Sometimes she even seemed to despise him. Sometimes he'd make jokes that weren't really jokes, and which didn't elicit any laughter, about how they hadn't had sex in however long. (It was a long time.) Even though, objectively speaking, he was a good dad and a commendable spouse. Their three mop-haired kids, two girls and a boy, were thriving, witty little humans, talented at sport and clever at school. He kept a good house. While they were at school, he read all the newspapers online and popular books about economic theory; you couldn't say he wasn't interesting conversation. But he knew he wasn't the sort of guy who looked really great on the arm of an oncologist. He knew his deprecating humour cloyed after a day of children dying of cancer. He was a fool, not an idiot.

Which was fine. He didn't belong in this house with the six bedrooms and five bathrooms and den and playroom and downstairs gym anyway. Okay, the gym was nice, all of it was nice, but it was a smothering sort of nice. He felt soft and dull there. He was becoming soft and dull. He joked about how someday, when it was all over, he'd certainly get laid, but he would never live with anyone ever again.

Now that the kids were all in school, he had started playing in the Brassica All-Star Brass Band. His bandmates were still pretty punk, all in their late thirties or early forties, but whose enduring devotion to anti-capitalism meant they lived in shitty walk-up apartments with unreliable girlfriends and rode fixed-gear bicycles. They bound their feet to the bicycle pedals with straps made of silver duct tape. They wore skinny black jeans and had sleeves of tattoos and earlobes distended by small discs of black wood. Those who had kids had more responsible wives with government jobs. Brassica's only gig, if you didn't count the odd children's birthday party, was playing a popular vegan restaurant on Friday nights.

Isn't that a bit loud in the end? Lola Stewart wondered aloud to him one day. The afternoon was sweltering, and they had stopped the game for a few minutes to drink the plastic-flavoured water they left in bottles by the side of the court. The gig was relatively new, and Jason was excited. She had eaten at this restaurant quite a bit; it was not a big space. The owners were Indonesian, and the place was cluttered with giant sculptures of Buddha and plastic trees. She tried to imagine an entire brass band fitting in somewhere.

Nah, said Jason, It's all good. Folks are chill.

But it was all good, too, because, in addition to playing with Brassica on Fridays, he had street hockey Sundays. For him, these two weekly events assuaged the sense that he was doing something wrong in the world simply by existing. Quickly, to his delight, the hockey games had taken on an air of political protest. They felt like an anti-gentrification F-bomb to the broader infilling currents of the neighbourhood.

The obvious contradiction was, of course, that Jason lived in one of the most gentrified instances of in-fill around, in a house that resembled a country manor, on a pie-shaped lot on the street closest to the river valley. When they purchased the property, they immediately tore down the previous house and built a home befitting his wife's social stature. Three storeys. Doric pillars on either side of the entrance because they reminded his wife of their honeymoon in Greece. They had marble countertops and plush light grey carpets that were professionally cleaned once a week. Before the children were in school, they had hired a Filipina nanny to help him out. (Three children under the age of five was too much for any one human.) But listen, his heart was protest. He solicited the renters, the misfits, the outsiders to play with him. He was still an underdog underneath it all.

So the weekly street hockey tournaments became, at least in theory, the underclass's rebel yell to the neighbourhood. They picked a bad patch of tarmac and, at first, hauled decrepit, off-kilter nets out of someone's garage. (Eventually, Jason had enough of this and bought good ones.) They solicited players from that rundown walk-up over by the park, renowned for renting to musicians, nay, whole bands.

Another two blocks over was a conspiracy of writers and painters, all also invited. At another, a literary translator, from English to Urdu, who was immediately in. His stickhandling was impressive. One of the guys had printed T-shirts during the early 2000s for one of the two NDP members of provincial legislature (also, the leader of the party): *Raj Against the Machine,* a fist in the air. They were all punk.

Lola Stewart was included because she was both an underdog (she was a renter, she was a single mother, she had a poorly paid but idealistic job), and her son went to school with one of Jason's children.

Lola Macbeth was invited because of the school connection. She certainly was not a renter. She, if you were to go down to brass tacks, also represented the sort of monied ease that the renters were rebelling against. But in the calculus of such things, she had recently begun to investigate her Indigenous identity, through her father that she had barely known, so that made her interesting. That made her an underdog. She was taking courses from the university for a certificate in Indigenous Sport and Recreation. She was learning about colonialism. She talked so much about colonialism, in fact, that those who with wobbly proclivities (who would swear sourly about the evils of land ownership at any opportunity, as if feudal Europe remained a resonant frame of reference in the twenty-first century) had plenty of opportunity to rehash one of their favourite critiques of land ownership. They liked that. Locke was wrong. Marx was right.

Of course, Macbeth was also really good at hockey. She moved with an irreproducible fluidity. She had such a sense of the game. Even at a fraction of her former glory, she elicited awe.

A fun part about the weekly tourney was also that, every now and then, Jason had everyone over after. This was bliss. Jason and his wife had one of those patios that was set up to be as comfortable as a living room. The seating had woven-plastic upholstery and was made of plastic recycled from milk jugs that was meant to look like wood. There was a shiny silver gas barbecue and a glistening hot tub. This all was surrounded by a pergola, protecting them from the heavens with a retractable awning. It was a vacation. Anyone's kids were welcome to come along; they could climb the trees in the backyard or launch themselves on the little custom-made climbing structure back there with real climbing holds, or undulate endlessly and screaming with joy on the wide swings hung from another massive oak tree in the back.

One such day, Lola Stewart changed into her swimsuit in the change room by the back, installed with showers, and grabbed one of the drinks from the fridge. She went out into the yard, heading for the hot tub.

Jesus, Lola, you're covered in bruises, yelped Jason when he saw her legs. How did this happen to you?

A rough game, I guess, she said, noticing that Sunday's new welts and discolourations for the first time. She adjusted the bikini she had recently bought on discount off the internet and descended, neck-deep, into the tub with the others. I think, she said aloud, that the Other Lola might have it out for me a bit.

But before she could say anything more, a bunch more people splashed into the tub, and then conversation shifted.

Because these were the renters, luxuriating, there was a dull squirm of body odour in the air. The talk turned to a murderer who had been scheduled to speak alongside a Black poet at a university the next province over. The Black poet was a legendary guy, someone who had fought racial injustice his entire career. He had worked with the murderer, thinking he was just a garden-variety criminal, maybe, who knows, to help him write poems. The Black poet was partially Indigenous himself. He was outspoken about the prison industrial complex. He believed in mercy. Unbeknownst to him, however, the murderer was a really bad man. He had murdered an Indigenous woman, awfully, and famously boasted about it afterwards. Not a garden-variety criminal at all. Actually, he was violent white male privilege doing its ruinous worst in the world. The murderer had gone to jail, after a spectacularly prominent trial, serving the time that he was told to spend there. Afterwards, he moved elsewhere and changed his name. Started writing poetry. The Black poet presumably believed in the second chance that those convinced of crimes should have. That those convicted of crimes and who have rehabilitated according to the terms asked of them, who served their time, have, in fact, redeemed themselves to society and should be forgiven.

At any rate, there was a massive backlash to the murderer coming back to read his poems. The murderer wasn't welcome in the community anymore. Those in the Indigenous community had said things like, we Treaty 4 peoples are trying to heal here and bringing his name to light is not helping us heal. That the Black poet should have consulted the members of the community about what he was going to talk about before coming to talk and bringing others to talk at the university. He should have made sure those topics were acceptable for the community beforehand. Instead, this.

The daughter of the victim, of the woman who had died horrifically, a death which was one of the first prominent instances of a murdered Indigenous woman in the sad pantheon of missing and murdered Indigenous women, spoke out. The daughter said: It's not fair the murderer gets to live a normal life, and even become a published poet, while my mother's life was cut short. He did what he did, he is who he is. He will always be that person.

I get that, Lola Stewart interjected into the rendition, I do. But what is the notion of justice that we are proposing in not allowing him to speak? Are we saying that the criminal justice system is nothing? Are we really comfortable that someone who has served his time, who has performed whatever amends that he has been directed to perform, can never be forgiven?

Yes, they're saying exactly that, snapped the Other Lola. His crimes are unforgivable.

It just sounds like any victim's family – they always want the criminal to be forever marked, forever tortured, replied Lola. But if we believe that someone who has been charged with a crime can never be rehabilitated, then what is the point of criminal justice? Are criminals categorically unredeemable? Because this is an attitude that harms – and in fact, does greatly disproportionate harm to – Indigenous offenders. Isn't this more a statement of Indigenous disempowerment within the criminal justice system? Shouldn't we be asking instead what a restorative or Indigenous-led system of justice might look like?

She assumed that everyone knew how much time that she spent working with Indigenous offenders, but this was an assumption. She could talk for ages about how difficult it was for her clients to find jobs after they finished serving time for whatever trumped-up charges that they had been slammed with in the first place. Whenever possible, judges tried to direct people into the systems for mental health, for drug addiction, for community service, which meant that a guilty plea would not result in a criminal record or jail time. But any contact with the system left a social scar if you weren't privileged to begin with. And what did the system, broadly, accomplish anyway?

Well, said Jason, jaggedly, the real problem here is that people aren't listening to Indigenous voices. It's just more white people trying to fix things. It's time for white people to shut the fuck up about this sort of thing and listen for once.

This met a smattering of applause from the mostly white, mostly tattooed, crowd. Someone uttered, Amen to that, brother. Macbeth reached across to bump fists with Jason.

But it's not like I'm oblivious to Indigenous notions of justice, retorted Lola, feeling the blood rush to her face. Her hot tub–pink face further pinkened. Jason, at least, knew how she spent her days. He had met her family. She interpreted this all as a specific critique of her views.

Thus, she continued: If the argument is that this guy, who I fully accept is probably a horrible and truly despicable human being, should be subject to Indigenous justice, then sure. That is also a system of justice. Let's talk about restorative justice. Let's talk about community accountability. Let's talk about Indigenous law and how it has survived colonialism's genocidal attacks and why we need to respect that as a robust and legitimate legal system. But the notion of irredeemability! From what I've seen, systems of justice which create irredeemable humans have rarely made them out of white bodies.

Other Lola fumed. She said: That is a totally colonial attitude to have. It's shocking to me that you would even think that you could utter such racist bullshit in my presence.

"In her presence" was a reference to Other Lola's Indigeneity. Last fall, she had started that certificate in Indigenous Sport and Recreation. (She took a part-time course load because it was too stressful to have to get her youngest to daycare and then for her to go to school all day.) Her biological father was Indigenous, and she had been learning about her ancestry. The Canadian history that no one had previously taught her. She had never heard of potlatches before, and how the government outlawed gift-giving, which was, in reality, economically essential to Northwest Coast First Nations. And it was unceded territory! And what about residential schools? The mass graves of Indigenous children, the intergenerational trauma. Her stepfather and mother were white, problematic colonialists, infuriatingly unaware of the gravity of her heritage. It was enough for them that she had grown up with the accoutrements of the upper middle class – the grandfather on her mother's side had won an enduring sort of riches from the Leduc No. 1, the 1947 discovery of oil that forged the province's old money class. Her mother had never needed to work. Her stepfather was an orthopaedic surgeon.

Meanwhile, her biological father ended up as one of those homeless alcoholics in the river valley. He had died of liver failure six years ago. She had seen him three times between when he left her mother, when she was a toddler, and his death. Anyway, Other Lola had a plan. When she was done, she was going to work at a large construction and engineering firm in town as a Traditional Ecological Knowledge consultant. She talked about it as if it were preordained, as if the job were already there for her and waiting to be claimed.

In the hot tub, talk wasn't quite sloppy yet. Most were still sipping at their first cans of beer. Lola was stunned by Other Lola's remarks and tried to remember that Other Lola's trajectory of human growth was not her trajectory of human growth, and that was okay. Sometimes, when your identity has been repressed for so long, when it has a chance to be seen, it comes out in spurts. So Lola just muttered, deferentially: Yes, you're right. I'm sorry.

Piles of kids were milling about in a ravenous sort of way; they had been given popsicles an hour ago, but that wasn't going to cut it any longer. At this point, the adults had been soaking in the hot tub for so long that they were uniformly purple. Their red faces exuded wet beads. Jason's wife appeared with Costco boxes of frozen burgers (beef, salmon, veggie) just in time. She set to work at the barbecue. Lola Stewart tugged at the bikini she had bought at discount and hauled herself out of the waters to use the washroom. She was hungry and thirsty and all the things. She hadn't seen her own children for an eternity.

In that special bathroom for those soaking in the backyard, Lola stood in front of the flatteringly lit mirror.

She was at once astonished by how salmon-coloured her skin was, how blackened her new bruises were, and, then, how transparent her new bikini was when wet. Wait, what? Who would make a swimsuit that was mostly transparent? She had just assumed that since it was lined – ugh. She recalled with a horrified feeling that this wasn't the first time that she had worn it, either. Two days ago, she had gone down to the community swim with the kids! She carefully rewrapped herself in her towel, a gauzy Turkish fabric that felt as whispery as the pale blue bikini's untruths about its essential bikininess, one of the towels that Jason and his wife kept rolled in a multicoloured heap in a wicker basket by the hot tub for anyone to use. Looking at her crimson face in reflection, she decided the highest road in this situation was to pretend that nothing had happened.

As she sauntered out, practising confidence, she found her son – his curls wet and plastered down, the kids having moved from the wading pool to play video games in the living room, goosebumps over his bare chest, a little bowl of orange goldfish crackers by his side – and whisper-hissed in horror to him: Why didn't you tell me that my swimsuit was see-through?

Oh, he said, barely looking up, I thought you knew that.

No! Of course I didn't know that! Why would I want to wear a see-through swimsuit?

It was confusing to me, too, Mom.

She left him to slip on a T-shirt and running shorts. Outside, Jason's wife was handling the barbecue alone. Stewart went to help assembling burgers and cucumber spears on plates for the kids. As they worked the production line together, Jason's wife goofed off, trying to make letters out of cut-up vegetables and lightly teasing with the little humans, famished and giddy, who were racing up. After the rush of food distribution, as the two women sat together on the edge of the porch with sparkly rosé in plastic glasses (now the children were onto ice cream bars and circulating wildly around the yard, hooting and ecstatic; it was the final stage of chaos before going home and to bed), Lola ran her toes through the perfect green grass. They're so alive, she muttered. Her daughter one-arm cartwheeled past, happily challenging a dare to eat a bite of ice cream while upside down. The late evening sun reassured, beaming through branches. Yes, agreed the doctor-wife. Her gaze bored knowingly into Lola's for a moment and then she continued. There is so much to be grateful for.

4. So well thy words become thee as thy wounds

Street hockey had a whole vocabulary to it. Lola Stewart relished the language. Deke. Dangle. Risk it for the biscuit. The words were infused with the scent of rubber shoes on blacktop. The two Lolas had been hustling (hockey of all sorts is all about the hustle, Lola Stewart had learned), and it always seemed that they were on opposite teams and responsible for defending each other. There weren't many women who played. They were vaguely within the same realm of ability, too, so this made a sort of sense. Which is to say, Lola Stewart had started off bad and was getting better. This was an increasing source of annoyance for Lola Macbeth. Sometimes Stewart would deke her out, or interrupt the Other Lola's progress towards her net, or pass the ball at just the moment that was unexpected. Other Lola didn't like this much. Consequently, she introduced Lola Stewart to the finer points of team competition: playing just a little bit dirty. Stewart had the easy-to-bodycheck-into-outer-space physique of a runner. The demonstrations were successful.

As a result, Lola Stewart found herself increasingly battered. Other Lola would accidentally check her, or trip her, or ram her stick into her ribs. The bruises came out later on Sunday evenings, truly blossomed on Mondays and Tuesdays, and began their slow, impressionistic healing Wednesday through Saturday. Then it was Sunday again and time to go play street hockey. Jason, who generally cared about this sort of thing, since aggression in sport was tangled in his complicated critique of capitalism, was impervious to the sheer stealthiness of Other Lola's tactics. After all, she had been trained to evade the eye of referees in world competitions.

This particular Sunday, Lola Stewart had managed to knock the Other Lola's stick, something that had previously only been done to her. She had succeeded in knocking the ball out of Macbeth's control and into her team's possession again. Lola Macbeth had cursed loudly. Sunbeams blazed all over the place. With a swift jab, the end of her stick went into Lola Stewart's face. Stewart, shocked that this was also what street hockey entailed, and also hurt, crumpled to the ground. The world swirled. Macbeth did not apologize. In fact, she sprinted after the ball as if nothing had happened at all. Lola Stewart thought at first it might have been an accident. But Macbeth was actually really good at hockey.

None of her other movements were accidental. She had gone to the world ringette championships four times when she was younger, after all.

So, on a particularly blossomy May afternoon, Lola Stewart found herself curled on the black tarmac. She cupped her hands under her face to catch cascades of blood pouring from her nose. More blood than she thought her face could have possibly contained. She desperately tried to remember if she should be pinching or tilting or – what *was* one supposed to do when one was bleeding like this?

Jason rushed over. Ugh, he cooed, observing the magnitude of blood, you've probably broken it. I'll get my wife to check you out. (She was in the playground with their children, not far away.)

As Lola waited, she observed how nothing really hurt. Her face felt wrong, and the blood was tremendous, more than she had ever seen leaving her body, except for maybe childbirth, but that experience was a long way from street hockey with friends and alleged friends on a Sunday afternoon. She had never broken her nose before. She could see that her elbows and knees were skinned, too, but yeah, numb. All of it. She crawled over to the grass and held her face. The game resumed, a little more gently, in that stunned, confused way that went a bit against inclination but triumphed insofar as there was no reason not to keep playing. What could anyone do?

The doctor-wife arrived and, using the flashlight on her cell phone to peer up into Lola Stewarts's nostrils, announced that she had broken her nose, but it wasn't a bad break. She wouldn't need surgery or for it to be set.

Definitely don't bother going into emergency, she announced after the inspection. You'd wait forever and there's nothing they can do. I'll call a friend at the sports medicine centre and see if she can get you in tomorrow just so she can double check, maybe prescribe some pain meds if you need them. What happened, anyway?

Lola Stewart wasn't quite sure what to say about what happened. I, uh, I don't know, she finally muttered. A stick to the face, I think.

The doctor-wife pursed her lips. Well, you're out of the game for a while now. Never a good idea to play with a broken nose.

And, as Lola hobbled home with her broken face, one of those instant ice packs pressed against her nose, those ones that turn grainy and cold when you pop the pellet on the inside, she still wasn't sure what to say. Blood streaked her T-shirt and her sneakers. She felt an urge to cry. When she got in the door, she realized she had forgotten to tell her children in the park that she had left. Someone else would let them know, she thought, while she searched for the Tylenol, washed her hands in the sink, tried not to look at her face in the bathroom mirror.

Later, after the kids had, indeed, returned home, only half-aware of what had happened, smelling of dirt and sunscreen and their toes dusted with sand, alive from that kid universe of play, the doctor-wife texted Lola. She wanted to check in, to give Lola the number to call tomorrow. How are you feeling, she asked. The attention was surprising. She was once again struck by how Jason characterized this woman and how this woman presented herself. What Lola wanted to ask the doctor-wife – she thought about this as she stood in the shower, not having responded to the text even though it would have been easy just to say that she was fine, as she tenderly lathered soap onto the rashes of blood on her knees and elbows and thigh – was whether she thought that she deserved it.

5. Unbend your noble strength

After she broke her nose, Lola's face turned into a crime scene. Her eyes turned purple, and her nose was yellow and puffy. She worked on disguises. The event confirmed to her and, she imagined, anyone who dared look upon her, that she was bad at makeup. She spackled concealer and colours on the opposite side of the colour wheel from her blue and yellow skin onto her face, a purely aspirational gesture prescribed by YouTube tutorials. The effect was ghoulish.

The sports medicine doctor had concurred with Jason's wife's initial assessment that the break was minor. Nonetheless. That doctor gave her a small run of weak painkillers and told her to avoid circumstances that might re-endanger her face for the next few weeks. This made sense. As she often felt when she did something banal but also catastrophic to her body, Lola was amazed by how unpleasant everyday injuries were. Her face was a catastrophe. She had a constant dull headache. Of course, her nose itself throbbed. The painkillers, as mild as they were, nonetheless instantly sent her to bed, where she'd stare at the ceiling, encased in a sort of amniotic bliss. Or she'd fall asleep and dream outrageously vivid dreams. This made taking them during work hours impossible, or at any time that she had to parent, so she didn't take them. Consequently, she always hurt. She wore outré sunglasses to school pickups – she didn't want to have to talk about it.

At work, she wasn't even sure what the protocol was about working with clients when she appeared as a recipient of domestic violence herself. Luckily, that first day when she went in, her superiors were out of the main office. She grabbed her binder and headed straight to her desk outside the courtroom. She kept the shades on for as long as she felt comfortable. But, and she probably should not have been surprised by this but she was, the clients were surprisingly sympathetic. More than one woman cooed, oh, honey, what happened?

Her favourite Cardinal was back, too, still not having submitted his application for Legal Aid, still in the midst of sorting out housing and rickshawing, and still wanting to have duty counsel roll over his appearance again.

Whoa, sister, he exclaimed when he finished his rote excuses and was ready to look at her, if not in the eye, but at least in that direction. What happened to your *face?*

Street hockey, Lola replied. He nodded, saluted her with two fingers, and ambled away. One of the amazements of this injury was that through the mythology of national sport, Lola had provided a complete answer.

As the morning ground on, her mind drifted, skimming over the ashtray acridness and veneer of alcohol in the air, and part of her considered taking pride in these wounds. She could puff her breast feathers of bravery, sport was a battlefield, not a figurative battlefield but an actual one, where something palpable and vivid was at stake. She could take pride in scars, damage, the irretrievability of perfect bodies. She was something special, a threat, she represented something formidable; she had form, and the form had force. These wounds were connection to a reality that transpired below the thrum of language and logic, a connection to the connections that were forged there. Right? But then her face throbbed again, hurt, and she knew she looked tired and beaten up and old. Her job was not to look this way, not to be this way. At that moment, another client came up to the desk, though, so she sat up straighter and tried to be normal. What else was she supposed to do? She didn't know.

The trip to collect children that afternoon was oppressive and exhausting. The afternoon sun creamed her headache. When she arrived at school, the children had already been let out of class and were trilling about the playground. She saw that Jason and the Other Lola were talking, but she had such a headache and was so tired. A quick wave hello, and then she slumped onto a bench and watched the children play. The sun beat down on her. She listened to the irruption of children's laughter, a babbling stream of life.

Then Jason was beside her on the bench. He was asking how she was feeling. She was wearing these saucer-sized sunglasses, purple acetate frames and blueish-purple lenses. The sand was greenish, and the sky shimmered unnaturally.

She looked over to him and muttered: I'm fine.

Right, he said. Well, I assume you're meant to be taking a bit of a break from the hockey tourney while you heal up, eh?

She nodded. Doctor's orders.

Right, well, um, so I was just talking with Mac, and, yeah. She, ah, wanted me to ask you to tone it down. Like maybe consider taking a break for the rest of the season. She thinks that you're too aggressive. Sure, I didn't see what happened, but I can't have these games turn into some kind of bloodbath every week.

Lola stared at him, straightening, feeling a bit of queasiness penetrate through the haze of fatigue and hurt. You realize, she said, that Lola Macbeth sticked *me* in the face?

Well, he said. She says it was an accident, and you were playing dirty. I guess you bled on her, and she couldn't clean out some of the stains, too. Listen, I don't want to take sides or be in the middle of this. But not everything needs to be a fight. You know this. You don't always have to disagree. I mean, some of your politics, I mean . . . they're . . . just not okay in all the places, you know? Mac is pretty sensitive about your stance on colonialism. Anyway, he said, exhaling deeply and clapping his hands on his knees. Kids gotta get home for snacks before they turn into monsters, amiright? Heal up, and let's talk in a few weeks about this.

He offered her a fist bump, and she didn't know what to do but to fist bump back.

She moved onto the grass, which was parched and yellowish, the dirt beneath that meagre thatch dry and hard, and lay down to stare at the sky. She thought about last winter, when the whole family went walking in the dog park. When they were all together, they were a lot of people. Counting heads, must've been almost a dozen. The winter day was mild, and the sun was strident on the snow. They blinked and wandered and pretended to adopt other people's dogs.

This was the game they played, something they had evolved years ago, Lola and the kids, when everyone wanted a pet but the house and Lola couldn't imagine having another creature to be responsible for either. It was fun. Walking through the field of off-leash dogs, each picked favourites and bonus points if you could convince it to come over for pets. That day, a stout brown bulldog followed her mother around for a while, trotting along at her heels. Because she was wearing a brown down jacket of almost the same shade, Lola and her sisters joked the dog had recognized a kindred spirit. Like those photo galleries of dogs and their owners, when the force of narcissism infiltrates pet affinity, the resemblance felt uncanny.

Then the man who appeared to be the dog's real owner, a bulky man in a buffalo-check wool shirt and ochre Carhartt's, a scruffy brown hipster beard exactly the hue of the dog's fur, claimed him. They strolled away together. Soulmates, announced Lola. Everyone agreed he was a better doppelgänger.

An airline was going bankrupt, someone said, and then someone was saying something about government handouts to the industry, the ethicality of such an ecologically selfish activity, and then the topic was airline travel in general.

Oh, but Papa is never going to fly anywhere ever again anyway, commented one of the sisters.

Lola wanted to know why.

The sister started to explain. After his mother had died, their stepfather had flown to Victoria to attend her funeral. Their stepfather, throughout this, walked stiffly off in the front. Lola wasn't sure if he wasn't listening or if he was beginning to be in a bit of a huff. But then he dropped back into the group, and she could see he was just waiting to interject.

It was a last-minute flight, he began, holding his hands out, ready for exposition. But, he said, the real problem was the fertilizer.

Lola started laughing. You tried to bring fertilizer on a flight?

No, no, said the youngest. The problem was that Papa had fertilizer residue on his hands and on his laptop! They caught it with that swab they use when you go through security.

Ugh, Lola thought. That was from his job. He tended to other people's yards. Landscaping. He was a landscaper. He flew with his driver's licence because he didn't have a passport. His last name was obviously Métis.

So what happened next? she asked. Somehow, she was still laughing. It was her faith in his storytelling; of course, the story would have a punchline.

Well, said their father in a deeper voice. They detained me.

Did you show them your best angles in the full-body scan? asked Lola. Or was it a cavity search?

There was a bustle of people approaching on the trail; there were so many people out. It was really kind of crazy. Global warming. You think it's just about warming temperatures, Lola said aloud, but it's also about unpredictable weather patterns. This is December?

This is actually a pretty clear-cut example of unambiguous warming, muttered one of the other sisters. They had moved into a single file line to let the others pass. Unseasonably warm winters, she said, might be what the planet needs to get the human species to pay attention at last.

No, said the youngest, it's never a good thing to be taken aside in airport security.

Does that mean cavity search? joked Lola again.

Their stepfather shook his head and started walking faster than anyone else. Lola kept laughing for a beat, they were all chuckling, but then she realized that nothing was remotely funny and, actually, the tears running down her face in the wind were just crying. Just before winter break, the day of the kids' holiday concert, but in the afternoon, her stepfather had been stopped again by the school janitor while trying to come into the school with Lola. It had been another fiasco of a day for her, and Lola's son, in Grade 2, had recently asked that Lola pick him up from school on time. When she was late to pick him up and all the other kids had been picked up by their parents, her son said, he sometimes forgot that she loved him. Ouch. Never mind that she wasn't often late, not truly last-kid-left-at-the-playground late. But she was almost never precisely on time. And it mattered. That day, things were dragging at work. She had pre-emptively called her stepfather to go to the school in case she wasn't there on time.

Then she was not late at all. She ended up meeting her stepfather by accident at the front doors, and they decided to go in together. Standing at the door when they approached was the custodian. He was an older Asian man, with an outdated uniform and thick plastic glasses that Lola was pretty sure dated from when her youngest sister was in school. Vintage. She knew this. He had been working there since forever. He certainly had seen her stepfather come in dozens, if not hundreds, of times before to pick up the youngest or Lola's oldest, who was in Grade 5. Yet today he stopped her stepfather. Demanded to know who he was, what he was doing trying to enter the school. He did this with the casual certainty of any security guard in the known universe, whose province was a small scope of absolute authority.

Lola stared at him witheringly. Said: He's with me. He's the grandfather of students here. Look at him. You recognize him. He's been picking up kids from this school for thirty years.

The custodian took a step back, and Lola pushed through. She was livid. Inside the school, though, her stepfather was apologetic. He confessed to Lola that he always waited for the kids outside. He could understand how the janitor might be confused or not recognize him. He didn't want to make a fuss. Lola watched him turn inside out with passivity and apology.

Now in the dog park, the bluebird sky and the blinding white snow, her eyes streamed with this wet rage. It was the wind, she told herself, mopping her face with a leather-palmed mitt, returning her attention to the branches of the trees, their comforting fractals against the crushed-up iceberg texture of the river, then to her family, trying to think of a joke that she could tell to make everyone laugh. But her mouth was dry, and so she instead just listened to the banter for a while. It was gentle, like a brook, against the reverberations of ice and snow; the others had processed this fresh rage already, it wasn't new to them as it was to her, and that fact was calming and eventually her rage wasn't her rage anymore but part of the landscape, something held outwards and ambient.

Back in the grass outside the school, against the decrescendoing babble of children on the playground as more of them began their migrations home, she decided it was time to go. She gathered the children. Fuck street hockey. Fuck her face. Fuck the idea of justice. Here is the here and now, she thought. On the walk home, the boy read from a joke book he had taken out from the library, endless bad jokes, mostly about animals. Why do you think children are always associated with animals? she asked him after the first eight jokes, why? Is it because animals don't talk and children when they are little don't talk, either? Is it because children are small, and some animals are also small? What about big animals? Do children have special insights into them, as well?

He ignored her steadily and read aloud in his patient small child voice: What was the first animal in space?

A dog. A Russian dog, Lola answered instantly.

He looked at her and smiled his sweet smile. No. Guess again.

His older sister, wiser: A chimpanzee?

Nope, he replied confidently. You want to know what it was? It was *the cow that jumped over the moon.*

Lola: That's not even true. It was a dog.

Sister, always already in the analytic mode: That's a nursery rhyme. Are they talking figuratively? But wasn't the cow jumping over the moon, like the moon was in the distance when the cow jumped? That's how I always understood it.

Lola: Not funny. Next.

Boy: Why shouldn't you visit a luxury wig shop?

Lola: Why?

Him: It's too high a price *toupée*!

Ha, said Lola. That one's okay.

The next joke wasn't funny though, nor the next nor the next. But he read the jokes aloud dutifully, still hopeful, not tripping into potholes in the back alley even as his eyes were elsewhere, and soon they were home. They were waiting for the sort of laughter that struck sometimes and was such a force between the three of them that their eyes welled with tears and their bodies shook with the reflex of it. They'd roll on the ground like fat monks and clutch their stomachs and sob in the transcendent pain of that much funny. Later, they elevated the activity to simply a game the boy called laughter yoga (was it really laughter yoga? none of them knew for sure; they just started calling it that), where he'd start laughing, and it spread to Lola and then the sister, laughing at nothing in tones that sounded fake at first but soon thickened and penetrated into their bodies, and soon grew uncontrollable powerful and genuine. If someone new to them was walking alongside and didn't know how to play, they'd walk up close to that person, one on each side and erupt furiously, and see how long it took for that person to start laughing with them. Not at, *with*. (Never that long.) But by the time they reached home, that game was still writ in cuneiform, with the reading of this book of unfunny jokes out from the library, which would soon be lost behind the couch for six months, and it had been another day of many details that more or less all faded from memory, even if they would remember some of them for quite some time.

An Antelope with a Bad Attitude

Diane hadn't eaten for days. She said her stomach hurt. That she must have a touch of the flu. The newspaper had said that the vaccine this year had been a poor fit for the virus going around, after all. Just a touch of something. She was resting in her bed, on maybe the third or fourth day, when her niece Annie came over. This was winter. Annie let herself in through the back door, didn't even ring. A gust of winter blew through the house. Willy, Diane's husband, reached for his bathrobe and mashed his cigarette into the ashtray on the coffee table in the living room. He tied the waist on the robe and stood up.

She was here to see Diane. Why. Willy didn't see the point. Diane would get better, she always got better. She just had a touch of something.

Outside, children had been released from the school across the street, a rupture against white snow. Little colours of snowsuits slipped over January. It was a commotion. Willy closed the door behind Annie.

Anyway, Annie insisted on it. She mounted the brown carpet stairs, treading on the darker brown track down the middle of each step. Willy went back to the couch and turned on Business News Network. His eyes traced the ribbon at the bottom of the screen announcing the TSX. He lit up another cigarette. Smokey rings puffed into the living room air.

Ten minutes later, Annie returned, her face flushed with anger. Her eyes bored blue at him. She hissed: She is not okay.

Things happened quickly after that. The ambulance came. Annie wasn't sure if Diane should be moved and was worried that she was breathing poorly, so she had called one. An ambulance came. Workers put her on a stretcher and connected her to oxygen and strung an IV into her ropey veins. Willy reached for a cigarette, feeling suddenly very disconnected, but one of the paramedics swatted it away. The oxygen, he snapped, could ignite.

—

At the hospital, in ER, the doctors discovered Diane had diverticulitis. The lining of her intestine had become infected and ruptured. She required immediate surgery. Willy noticed Diane wasn't that awake anymore. She looked far thinner than normal. Her skin was leathery, falling in on itself into wrinkles. She wouldn't stay awake. How had he not noticed this earlier? He had thought that she was just tired.

Annie, in contrast, was livid. Her cheeks were red, her eyes all glare. She disappeared to call the rest of the family: Diane's sister, Joyce, who was Annie's mother, and the nieces, who were Joyce's other three children. Diane disappeared into surgery. Willy walked across the street and bought coffee from Tim Hortons. He smoked outside alongside the heart patients and fresh amputees, all grey-faced and with IVs trailing their wheelchairs. Furtive young doctors in scrubs smoked half cigarettes. Willy waited. He had time.

The doctors couldn't complete the surgery. Technically, Diane died on the operating table, but they managed to revive her. Stitched her back together. Put her into ICU. Willy went deep inside the hospital to see her, where everything felt subaquatic. They had been swallowed into the belly of the beast. In the dark and blue-walled ICU, it was always nighttime; thoughts were always submerged. Willy was a blur. She looked dead. What did dead look like? Anyway, she was so thin. The life support machinery, tubes and orifices, whispered her chest up and down on the bed.

On the second day, she tried to pull out the breathing tube. Willy thought this meant she'd be okay. She had a fighting spirit. The nurses tied her arms down to the edges of the bed so she wouldn't do it again. This wasn't, he reasoned, something that they would do to someone who was dying.

The family flocked.

She was such a good swimmer when she was young, Joyce reminded everyone. Joyce looked like Diane, but she was not as thin. Her hair was a thick grey that she tucked behind her ears, framing a red face and wet blue eyes. Tennis, too. Such an elegant tennis player. Before she got too frail. Joyce was also convinced that Diane would get better. She sat beside the bed, her grey hair tucked behind her ear, stroking Diane's cheek, whispering, You're strong. You may be thin, but you are strong. Diane's eyes fluttered open sometimes. She couldn't speak with the breathing tube in. A tear rolled down her cheek.

The day after that, the doctors tried again. This time, they were able to complete the operation. Able to remove part of her intestine. A healthy person, one of the doctors announced, would have a seventy percent chance of surviving this. But because she didn't take care of herself, the odds are not quite as good. But they are still not that bad.

Nonetheless she was getting better. Day by day. Rousing back to herself, daily.

She needed to eat. The doctors kept saying this. The refrains summoned images in Willy's mind of huge roasts and gold wine goblets, like a nursery rhyme feast or something out of a cartoon: blackbird pies, apples, mashed potatoes, stuffed squash, cornucopias of fruit and cheese. A fat king helming the table, fat ring-encrusted fingers clasped over his belly. Is that how it worked?

Meanwhile, he went out for cigarettes, again amongst the wheelchairs, the IVs, hospital gowns flapping gauzily in the cold air, those rushed, embarrassed doctors. He shuddered in the cold. His lighter kept blowing out in the wind tunnel between the brutalist brick buildings, the four square metres of designated smoking area.

One day, when returned to her hospital room, the rest of the family was there again. Diane was awake now. Diane wasn't quite the same as she had been before; she was more wizened and less witty. While she was dead, she had had these dreams that she wanted someone to write down. And what happened when she slept, you wouldn't believe. One of the nieces had brought a notebook. Willy half-listened to these recitations, fragments about clouds and monsters and tunnels; they were like any dreams, vivid nonsense. Diane had never taken any drugs before, and now she was on a morphine drip.

Eventually, they turned to cracking jokes.

What do you call an antelope with a bad attitude? asked the eldest of the nieces, a wicked smile on her face.

A cantaloupe! cheered her little children. Obviously, they had heard this one before. The spontaneous laughter of children was a carbonation that bubbled to the space of the room.

What do you call two fruits who can't get married?

Cantaloupes! cheered the children again.

Hey, wait . . . said another niece, thinking for a moment. Then speaking slowly: What do you say when you don't want to go to your aunt's elaborate wedding?

Can't elope?

The niece shook her head.

Joyce looked devious. Her blue eyes glimmered. Aunt, elope! she cried. She beamed triumphantly.

Or what about three lesbian mistresses? offered Willy. What would you say then?

The comment spun out into an immediate silence. The jubilance which existed despite the tubes and electronic monitoring, despite Diane's twig-like legs poking ridges beneath blankets, despite that Diane herself was a skull and twigs and pulsing veins and sinews beneath a parchment of skin, her reddish crimped hair haloed around this skull on a blueish pillowcase, suspended the comment in midair. Everyone wanted the joke to be a joke. But his words spun into nothing.

Um, what? asked one of the nieces finally.

Uh, it's, uh, that she can't elope, right?

No one laughed. Diane looked up. Her thin lips pursed a polite smile. Willy understood that she was at least proud of him for trying. He could tell she appreciated his humour.

Diane died. Three months after the diverticulitis, Willy awoke in the night, and she was in some sort of seizure. He called the ambulance, and they kept her from dying on the spot. In the emergency ICU, one of the same nurses was working as the first time they had gone in. This nurse cried when Diane was moved to the palliative ward, or whatever it was called. Some section of the hospital that was a euphemism. Willy had never realized it was, really, where the dying people go to die. Dying in the short term. He had never seen a nurse cry before. Her face scrunched up ugly and flushed as the elevator doors closed, as they took Diane on the moving bed, now untethered from all the machinery, to this other section of the hospital.

What had happened was this. She hadn't been gaining weight. The doctors kept telling her to eat, but everything upset her stomach. Everything would be better if she ate, they had told her. If she just *took care of herself.* But she couldn't. Now, in the hospital again, a scan revealed that her intestines had perished. So that was why she had no appetite. She hadn't had a heart attack, but a heart event. But it didn't matter at that point because her intestines were already dead. The hospital workers put her on life support until the whole family arrived. Then they would take her off life support and wait for her to die.

He – or she, he couldn't figure out – was assigned a social worker. As the family assembled, trickling in one by one from whatever they had been doing with their mid-afternoons, the social worker kept insisting, in her neutral tones, she will not recover from this. She is dying. She will die very soon.

Why does she keep on saying that? asked the niece who had arrived first. She had heard the spiel four times already. Willy shrugged. Then he went for a cigarette break, and when his fellow smoker – a farmer in his mid-fifties, maybe, cowboy boots and Wranglers and plaid, his skin sun-weathered, he didn't belong in the city but his wife was recovering from gall bladder surgery – chatted him up, Willy confessed that he was waiting for his wife to die.

No, this man announced. His bronze, machinery oil fingers gestured with the cigarette a side-to-side negative. Do not give up hope.

But she doesn't have an intestinal tract anymore. She cannot survive. How would she eat? Willy reasoned.

You just have to believe in miracles, the cowboy insisted. He then recounted how many times his wife had had cancer. Thyroid then breast then uterus. Those doctors had told them she'd die so many times, but she kept not dying.

She's just got one boob left, and they think it's got the cancer now, too. But I believe in god. God has a plan. God can make miracles happen.

After she was taken off life support, it took Diane much longer to die than anyone expected. Twelve hours. Until four in the morning. She never regained consciousness. Joyce tucked her grey hair behind her ears and told jokes and stories, cried, then told more stories, and then conversation got lost again in family banter – everyone hadn't assembled in one room since the last time that Diane had been in the hospital. Throughout it, Joyce wouldn't let anyone say anything too dispiriting. In case Diane could still hear. She'd lean in close, stroking Diane's soft, wrinkled forehead, and whispered.

Willy had never been present when someone died in a hospital before. The nurses meted the morphine exactly. They didn't want the opiate to slow her breathing too much. But her breathing was slowing because she was dying. He watched the muscle on her neck, the one that would tighten if she were in pain, intently.

And when she died, she evaporated. You see people die in the movies all the time. But they never transform. He didn't expect the softness to disappear so quickly, like a receding tide. An ungraspable thing leaving. Such a rapid metamorphosis to wax. He didn't know that humans did that.

After Diane died, Willy bought a new car. A gleaming white BMW convertible. He liked to ride it around the neighbourhood feeling the wind blow in his hair. How surely it accelerated under his foot!

He saw Joyce one day, stopped her in her Prius beside him a red light. He pretended to be engrossed in programming his radio. When the light turned, he pushed his glasses back up on his red nose and rocketed past. Vroom.

His neighbours, Fred and Jennifer, invited him over for dinner. He suspected they felt sorry for him. Fred was a university professor. Political philosophy. Like Willy, Fred had a shaggy, mousey-brown moustache. Jennifer had been Fred's grad student. Now she was his second wife.

When he had taken early retirement from his IT job at the university, some three years before Diane died, Willy's days had spilled open. He had never noticed the texture of sunlight on weekday mornings: thin, unwitnessed. Diane had always kept busy, but his time cracked apart to emptiness. He drew the blinds open, and, for a while, he became a watcher of signs. The circulations of children to the school across the street. The nannies arriving at the community league's playgroup on Tuesday and Thursday mornings, small humans in tow. Grey-haired retirees strolling their dogs down the street to the dog park.

And, of course, he watched his neighbours' houses. It didn't take him too long to become bored of this – he decided to start trading stocks online instead – but during this brief time, a few years back, before Diane died, he witnessed some eruption next door at Fred's house. The lights were left on for all hours. Gesticulations in the kitchen. Then moving trucks. The first wife disappeared. Fred laid low. Willy lost five thousand dollars online. Sometimes he saw Fred's kids, their teenage scowls blotchy and resolute, let themselves in the back door. Willy lost seven thousand dollars.

Nonetheless, Willy had observed this trading of the spouses with interest. Fred's first wife had refused makeup, had left her shock of white hair conspicuously undyed. She was also a political science professor in the same department as her husband. Her hair was all the way down to her waist.

Not long after the first wife had packed up and left, Jennifer arrived. It was spring. She had chestnut brown hair that was glossy and alive. She wore makeup. Jennifer was thirty-five. She liked to entertain. The invitations started arriving before Diane died, but Diane was such a picky eater. And so shy she talked herself out of letting Willy accept. Now things were different.

So, the Wednesday after the Thursday that Diane had died, he made his way out the front door, across the dead snow to the house next door. His shoes crunched in the thick grains of snow mottled with black. Melted and refrozen snow was glum. It was mostly dark already, and it wasn't even 4:30.

He thought how Diane had started teaching exercise courses for senior citizens after her own mother had died. No, she had started by *taking* those classes, he remembered. She was in her forties when her mother had died, and she had started taking classes intended for seventy-year-olds. Because it was ridiculous for her be taking those classes, she had graduated to an instructor almost immediately. How she mourned her mother was to become old like her, psychically, even though she wasn't physically. But then she died, too young. So maybe she had been right all along.

Without thinking, he rustled through the pockets of his parka, found his cigarettes and popped one between his lips. Then, remembering that neither Fred nor Jennifer smoked, and likely didn't permit it in their house, he took a few fast puffs and tossed it back over towards his front porch. As he was walking, his bad leg, the right one, caught in a snow drift. He nearly lost his balance, then did one of those theatrical skitters across the walk. He righted himself again.

Fred and Jennifer's house was tasteful and warm. Poured concrete floors and amber lighting. The humidity of boiling pots and roasting meat filled the air. Jennifer brought him wine. Willy sat and massaged his sore leg. Fred turned on the fireplace. He had recently had a hip replacement – years of running marathons had damaged the joint somehow; he was, he swore, one of his doctor's youngest patients ever – and was still limping around with a crutch. He had the lithe body that Willy associated with runners, though he was much taller than the little Black men that won all the races. Fred expressed sympathy for Willy's hurt leg.

For a few minutes, Willy watched the flames of the gas fireplace flicker. In the days since Diane had died, he had discovered the details of her death didn't seem that important. Saying them aloud made him tired. What was done was done. Jennifer and Fred didn't want to talk about it either, he could tell. Once they sat down to eat, however, Willy felt compelled to mention it.

Magazines, Willy finally blurted, with what he thought was appropriate scorn. He stopped cutting a piece of roast into a tiny triangle and set down his knife beside the plate. What he said was a non sequitur. Jennifer had been talking about a traffic calming pilot project in the neighbourhood. Unrealistic beauty ideals, he continued aloud. Women get sucked into it, and then they can't escape. He took a deep sip of wine. He realized that Jennifer and Fred were staring at him, expecting him to say more.

When I remarry, I'll pick someone who doesn't have those sorts of hangups.

Jennifer raised an eyebrow. Do you have someone picked out already?

Oh no! But, you know, I'm just assuming. I'm still young, after all.

Not the next morning, but the morning after, Willy woke up feeling as if he had the flu. He was meant to meet Diane's best friend since high school for brunch, but he called her to cancel. Sitting up felt awful. He didn't trust himself to walk to the washroom. A sense of malaise was lodged on his chest. He mentioned this while talking to Diane's best friend on the phone, who insisted that she come over and check on him. She could bring soup. She missed Diane, too. He indulged her. Told her the code for the back door, so that she could let herself in. His head spun thinking of walking all the way downstairs and to the back door.

When she arrived, Willy was so disoriented that he thought for a moment it was Diane. They had the same tall, slight build, reddish-brown hair, the same frenetic motions when they were nervous. She called 911. She fluttered her hands. When the paramedics arrived, they credited her with saving his life. They told him that he had had a massive heart attack. He was lucky to be alive.

He spent a week in hospital, where the doctors ran tests and informed him that he also had severe coronary artery disease. The pain in his leg was because his femoral artery, that one running down his leg, had been completely blocked. But, his dark-eyed doctor told him, a young Asian woman whom Willy found utterly alluring, gesturing with her pointer finger towards the sky, or where the sky would be were they not in Cardiac ICU, the body is a wonderful machine. It grew tiny new arteries and veins. But they do not work quite as well as the original ones. She insisted that he promise to quit smoking: I've heard people say quitting smoking is like killing your best friend. You've had that emotional support for decades, that release to turn to. But this, she gestured with her index finger again, this time to the mess of tubes and wires, is pretty strong motivation to start living a healthier lifestyle.

He agreed easily to all of this. His will felt pliable. He knew, deep down inside, he wouldn't miss cigarettes. He was one of those tubular inflatable men by the side of the road, flapping and collapsing in the wind but enduring, indefatigable, eternal.

When Willy returned home, he found four speeding tickets in his mailbox. He hadn't had a cigarette in the seven days since he had been admitted to the hospital. He had never gone this long before without smoking. His tongue felt fresh. His tastebuds felt like new flowers. Pink. Blooming. Pushing open the oak front door, he was able, for the first time, to appreciate how pungently the house smelled. Mostly of ashtray and Diane's chewing gum. Wrigley's double mint. He tossed the tickets onto the sideboard by the front door. The house felt bigger, flatter, filled with space and dust motes. He changed into his bathrobe, emptied all the ashtrays, and sought out his spot on the couch. He turned on the Business News Network. There was a debate going on about the dropping price of oil.

Now that he wasn't smoking – this was one of those moments where he most certainly would have lit up a cigarette, and he felt a strong sudden tingle of missing something – he observed how his skin had turned pink and blotchy, as if it had been inflated with air and then shrunk again. It had a strange luminosity. Pinker than he had ever seen it, but somehow chalky. It had been peeling for several days now. Little squares of skin kept tumbling off. He was moulting. Willy wondered how long this would go on. He suspected he had endless layers to shed.

The next day Fred called. He had heard about Willy's heart attack and was wondering if Willy wanted to do rehab with him. Just walking around the block together, slowly, maybe working up getting all the way over to the top of the river valley in time, a mile away. Fred had plans to get back to running, but it would be a while before he could do that.

Willy said yes.

When Joyce called later to see how he was doing, he told her that he had started training for a marathon with Fred. Fred's resting heart rate was thirty-five beats a minute. That's the sort of guy he was training with. Good things were going to happen, he told her. He could feel it.

—

The next day was uncharacteristically warm. One of those mid-winter melts. The sun was brilliant off the snow, enough to make his eyes ache. Willy met Fred on the sidewalk outside, at the dividing line of their property. He wore his hiking boots, stiff still from years ago when Diane had insisted that he have good footwear to walk with her after dinner. She walked with arms swinging, her elbows jutting out. He hadn't been able to keep up. He hadn't even broken the leather in. His boots were shiny, too. Shiny boots for a shiny day.

Global warming, announced Fred. People think that it's about the planet getting warmer, but really it's about unpredictable weather patterns.

The sound of wet slurried through eavestroughs. The spruce out front dripped. The asphalt sidewalk glistened wet and promisingly.

Well, said Willy. Every day is a blessing, after all.

Baby Brain in a Vat

Adele, surrounded by three friends and three glasses of wine into the evening, was holding court at the pizzeria. She paused for a moment mid-sentence and sat up straighter. She turned her face towards the filament light bulbs, those fat Edison ones, hanging naked over the raw wood tabletop. Over there, a pizza kiln was stoked with wood. It glowed molten orange, the centre of the sun. Endless bottles of craft beer lined up against the wall. She really had picked the right place for her night out with the girls and, anyway, the point is that Adele's husband was smart. Like, really smart. He was a professor at the university. His position as Canada Research Chair in Clean Energy and Sustainable Mineral Resources had just been renewed. This was what had happened since the last time she had seen the others. It was a big deal.

Sure, she confessed, of the million or so dollars that the grant represented, they as a family would pocket almost none, but that wasn't the point. People didn't understand this about university grants. It all went to other people's salaries, field projects, equipment, et cetera. It wasn't money that they themselves would receive. They wouldn't be rich! The meaning of his CRC chair was the acknowledgement he didn't study something abstract or unimportant. His work was important to the future of humanity. It had been featured in the media, even American news programmes.

Adele had booked a table for eight at this place, which was not so far from their school, but only four had shown up. In their going-out clothes, faces thick with makeup, women who didn't leave the house enough. Outside, it was February and raining. Adele disliked all of them. She didn't know why she had bothered, except she, too, needed to leave the house. The wine was helping. She felt her cheeks flushing red. The pizza hadn't arrived yet. Adele suspected she wouldn't have an appetite when it finally did.

But I didn't marry Cody because he was going to be successful, she heard herself continue, don't think that I was conniving like that. I married Cody because he was funny. He always could make me laugh. And I liked his smile.

The other mothers nodded blankly. Yes, one agreed finally, the one who came to their house periodically for dinner with her own academic husband, actually, he was just a teacher at the technical school in town, he didn't even have a doctorate, and their three boys. They knew that the Cody she had married was now balding and thick in the middle, and that no one laughed at their house anymore. Yes, this woman said again, generously, I could see that.

The reason no one laughed or told jokes or was jovial at Adele's house was an open secret. The women, Adele knew, didn't dare bring it up. Something was wrong with their daughter. Adele had three children, two boys, ten and eight, and then a daughter, Tuuli, who had just turned three. Tuuli was blond and blue eyed and beautiful, and something was wrong with her. What it was exactly that was wrong, no one knew. She didn't walk or talk and couldn't feed herself or do any of the things that three-year-olds should be able to do.

While there were undoubtedly other warning signs, which better or more attentive parents would have noticed earlier, Adele only suspected when Tuuli was maybe six months old. That was when Tuuli started screaming and screaming every time she soiled her diapers. Then she started screaming before anything happened. These shrieks bore through Adele's ears and somehow failed to distress Cody to any actionable degree. Thus, it was inevitably Adele who would rush over and pick her up and race to the bathroom and strip off Tuuli's clothes and hold her over the toilet. Then it was okay. It was cleaner anyway. But when they were driving, or out somewhere where she couldn't do this, Adele would just have to listen to her. She disliked the sound of children crying. It rattled her on the inside. Cody, who somehow endured it, pointed out that women are simply biologically inclined to be more bothered. And even as you go deaf, he pointed out in his lecturing-to-students voice – as if Adele was going deaf, she *wished* she were going deaf, but no, she was not – the pitch of an infant's shriek is always the last to go.

Neither of her other children were like this. They were boys who charted the easy progress outlined in the pamphlets at the nurses' clinics. Height, weight. Milestones. Their dotted-line curves were buoyant promise. One blond, one brown-haired. They were growing up to be good at school, at sports. At life. Nonetheless, between the boys' hockey games and soccer games and cello lessons, sitting in the chilly stands or a camp chair or a lumpy velour armchair, Adele tried not to think about how much time she had spent holding babies over toilets or listening to children scream. Of course, it was really just the one child. But that one distorted everything.

By day, Adele was an interior designer. Or she had been. Sometimes people would slip up and call her an interior decorator, but really the two things were very different. Interior designers had to go to university, and, even if it wasn't quite the same sort of schooling as architects, they were certified by the same provincial agency. Interior designers could take down walls, change the interior architecture of the building, sign off on structural plans. In contrast, interior decorators were the ones on HGTV, catering to depressive housewives who liked to spend their husbands' money on cloying paint jobs and cheap light fixtures. *This* was why interior designers weren't taken more seriously. *This* type of woman. Some of the women in Adele's company – yes, they were also all women – thought about lobbying to have the profession's name changed to "interior architects." They would be taken more seriously. They really did build things.

Tuuli was born as her babies are born, in a squat of blood and deep-gouged (but ultimately forgettable) terror, and Adele insisted that they name her after a family friend who had died of ovarian cancer two years earlier. Tuuli meant "wind" in Finnish. Adele liked this. She was happy to have a girl. Tuuli's early life started off familiarly, too. Adele, who never really stopped working, carried her to meetings in her car seat, and she was so quiet; babies that age are so easy. After Tuuli was born, and Adele had taken these six months of maternity-ish leave, she and Cody put her into the infant daycare on campus. It was the same daycare where they had put the boys, and where some of Cody's colleagues had put their kids. It was supposed to be a good place. They had never had problems. No one had had problems.

The workers, typically, were firmly lodged on the other side of that gulf of social disparity, of class or race. Women either with terrifying teeth and ill-advised tattoos who stank of ashtray or new Canadians who were undoubtably astrophysicists or economists in their motherland. Both demographics had universally bored affects around the children, even though this was an allegedly top-notch early childhood education facility, a not-for-profit centre affiliated with a university. Every employee had to have certification in early childhood education. It was a post-secondary diploma! Cody complained about the cigarette stench, but not Adele. She wasn't surprised. What did he expect? What woman would want to do that sort of work if they hadn't made mistakes in life? These workers, predictably, didn't like Tuuli's screaming routine around shitting. This was another thing for Cody. He had gone to pick her up one day, and Tuuli had been sitting in a dirty diaper. How, he asked, and Adele found the comment a bit rich, could they tolerate the noise?

And later, when their pediatrician had prescribed some physiotherapy exercises, since at that point Tuuli was fifteen months old and showed no sign of learning how to stand up by herself, let alone walking – she had just dropped off the progress charts for all this sort of thing altogether – the daycare workers refused to do them with her. It was so infuriating. Adele brought the exercises on a sheet of paper for them, with little pencil-drawn stick figures in various poses representing Tuuli. All it was was doing things like helping her to stand up, say at the sand table, three times a day. Nothing complicated. Tuuli liked the sand table! It wasn't hard. The workers, all women, all obstinate, simply said they were too busy. Meanwhile Cody fumed. Why were they called early childhood *educators*? he asked. Bullshit.

They decided that Adele should take an extended leave of absence from work. With all Cody's new accolades and the fact that he was on the cusp of being mid-career, he earned triple Adele's income. Even though Adele was half owner of her interior design company. She told everyone it was so that she could ensure Tuuli was getting her physiotherapy in. That it was just until they figured out what was going on and got her onto the right track again. Up to speed. She spoke of rectifying Tuuli in all of these sports metaphors, and Adele hated sports. But it was her choice. She said a lot of things to avoid saying that she was quitting work, because she knew that was exactly what she was doing. Quitting work. To be a stay-at-home mother to a disabled child. She and her business partner had planned to sell the company to an architectural firm, the offer had been sitting on the table for quite a while, so they did that. Really, everyone knew exactly what was happening. It wasn't her choice. Adele took the money and planned a multitiered garden for their front yard.

At the pizza place, the other women were talking about this and that. They had so much passion for things. One had spearheaded a campaign to have chocolate milk removed from the lunch milk programme. She was enthusing about it. One cup of chocolate milk had twenty-six grams of sugar in it. That was five teaspoons of sugar! Think about how much sugar the children were not consuming now that they drank two percent at lunch now. The woman, an Australian whose husband had come to work at the new heart clinic associated with the university, pointed her index finger upwards as she spoke and shook it back and forth. As it had happened, the principal of the school, when served with the petition the Australian had submitted, immediately consented to the ban. Just like that!

Another mother at the table asked what the sugar content was in normal milk. The Australian didn't know. But, she added, another thing: carrageenan. Chocolate milk contains carrageenan. It's banned in Europe. It's a known carcinogen.

Then the pizzas arrived, weird creations all. The waiter announced them as he set them down. *Uva arrosto,* grapes roasted with rosemary, pine nuts, and goat cheese. *Patata e pancetta,* potatoes, rosemary, mozzarella and an egg on top. *Gamberi,* tiger prawns, flor di latte, lemon zest, fennel, and horseradish. Adele slugged the remainder of her wine and motioned to the waiter for another carafe. While they were eating, the chubby mother said that she hated it when people stared at her eating just because she was fat. Like fuck off already. Fat people eat. No one else at the table was fat, so what followed was one of those pauses where no one knew what to say.

Adele, however, picking around the uvas, shrivelled and charred, half raisins, realized she agreed. It's like how much I hate it when I'm out with Tuuli and people stare and I hate it, she blurted. But a wise friend of mine told me – this was actually Tuuli's physiotherapist, but Adele thought of her as a friend; it's not like she could talk about these things with many people anyway – that it's not *my* responsibility to make those around me comfortable.

Amen to that! cheered the other mom.

Despite the alcohol, despite this simmering loathing that constantly brewed beneath her skin, Adele meant this. She had been trying to think like this. Cody had started staying at work later and later, showing up perfunctorily just in time to take the boys to their activities, now hockey and tennis and cello. Then the summer he was in the field with his grad students, all over the western provinces and the north, as he was every year. Whereas beforehand Adele had taken the boys to visit sometimes, it didn't make sense now. Not with Tuuli and all her appointments. And think about the stroller. You couldn't take that out into the field. Lugging Tuuli wasn't an option either: she was too heavy. Adele had plans to take the kids down to her parents' ranch in the foothills instead, a little ranch in the rolling hills, variegated green. Beyond that, the bluish-tinted mountains. This is where Adele had grown up, and her parents liked the kids well enough. Good enough for a vacation. While the other families at school toured the French Riviera or Copenhagen or the Sistine Chapel. Adele wasn't going to talk about it.

Adele had taken to calling Tuuli her "baby brain in a vat." Tuuli's former nickname, her "cutest accident to date," had started to seem unkind. This is not to suggest that Tuuli was not an accident. She emphatically was. And Adele was not one of those women with stretch marks clawed against a permanently distended stomach, the sort who would smartly correct mothers at playgroup when they used the phrase "accident" like that. Adele who prided herself on being exactly the same 5'5" and 120 lbs at forty-three that she had been at thirty-three! These women moralized clichés like: there are no accidents, only *unplanned pregnancies*. Or *surprises*.

These were the same sort of women who talked about bundle of joys as if they were the first humans to hold a swaddled baby. The ease they had in their bodies terrified her. But Tuuli was, after seventeen years of her parents' increasingly chaste cohabitation and one night at a particularly port-infused dinner party at the house of Cody's department chair, entirely an accident. Sorry. It was a fact independent of love.

The vat was the surprise. The vat was the car seat and, later, the strollers.

Or the vat was the endless appointments with doctors, so vast. The genetic testing that Cody refused and then accepted, which revealed nothing anyway. One specialist thought it was tethered cord syndrome, when the spinal cord has tissue connecting it to the spinal column and so things don't move or connect as they should. This would have accounted for Tuuli's weakness in the legs, but not for her weakness everywhere else. But tethered cord syndrome could be fixed by surgery, so Adele sent an email to her family and closest friends announcing that Tuuli could be fixed. It was the most jubilant she had felt for months. She had been forty when Tuuli was born, after all. But after she clicked "send," a second specialist wanted additional testing. That testing then showed it wasn't tethered cord. Adele, prickled by her idiotic optimism, wasn't sure what to say in a follow-up email, so she didn't send one.

The vat was Tuuli's body. This was obvious, the thing no one said aloud. Tuuli who looked Adele in the eye and moved her mouth when Adele took her from the crib in the morning, it looked as if she was chewing, but eventually Adele realized that this is what Tuuli thought talking was.

Apart from screaming, which had developed various tones, happy or scared or angry et cetera, Tuuli didn't talk. Just eye contact and this chewing motion. She was so intent, fat cheeks and those blue eyes, when she moved her mouth and did not talk. What was she saying?

These pretend conversations moiled in Adele's chest. Her breath suctioned under the strain of so much broken-feeling love. This was proof that Tuuli had an internal life and it was mostly unknowable. Tuuli recognized Adele and Cody and the boys and their friends. She preferred this toy over that toy. When they took her to dinner at other families' houses, which they did only on very rare occasions with trusted friends, Adele struggled not to take personally this thesis that Tuuli's appearance proposed of vacancy. Chewing her mouth sometimes and flapping her arms, but usually just staring off into space. Eventually Adele realized that Tuuli was bored, and that Adele would be bored, too, in the same situation, but that in itself was hardly an actionable revelation. Adele was not in the same situation. What was Tuuli thinking about? What would bring her joy? Until recently Adele thought a tenet of parenting is understanding your children, in that mysterious genetic sense of knowing, and that, with minor modifications, had been her experiences thus far. The boys were of her. She understood their predilections, their geekiness, their introversion, their humour without having to make an effort. But Tuuli, no. Tuuli's dreams were opaque, instead borne of hours of muscle spasms and screams.

For her part, Adele's dark thoughts eventually tumbled to dualism and blame: Tuuli's body was molecularly, genetically, essentially at fault. The scientists didn't have a word for it, either. No matter how many appointments or specialists they consulted. No matter how many conjectures about obscure syndrome this or that. No matter how much parsing the probability of genetic influence or the blatant rareness of this mystery. This was a brokenness inseparable from Adele's own. This meant that Adele, too, was essentially flawed. The doctors, purveyors of Hallmark reassurances, told her not to blame herself. But how else could she have made this unwalking, untalking human being? Who had the atrophied legs and arms too unpredictable for her to feed herself. Whose jaw hung slack most of the time, even if the corners were typically upturned into a compelling half smile. She feared, in creating a human, she had also created prison.

The waitress brought another carafe of wine to the table. The woman whose husband wasn't a real professor, the one who taught kids about robots at the polytechnic in town, shrieked a little. This was grating, how she always talked about how much she loved to drink wine but then she'd pour a quarter glass and then pour sparkling water in, nearly to the brim. This was her idea in the first place, to get the moms out for wine night. Seriously! This woman held the preposterously full glass up to toast the others. Her teeth were nonetheless a ghoulish purple when she smiled. Adele grinned back, lips carefully closed, and held her glass up to the others. Clink.

One time after Tuuli's therapeutic swim sessions, at the swimming pool across town where special courses were run for children like her, in the pool that was deliberately kept warmer than the other swimming pools, Adele saw in the showers afterwards an enormously pregnant woman, naked and meticulously scrubbing herself with soap. She must have been one of the other mothers. Anyway, Adele couldn't stop looking at her. It was grotesque. What struck her first was how completely she herself had forgotten pregnancy. The sense of it in her body was gone. Expanding, stretching, that becoming strange to oneself. Dimensions became hyperbolic. The experience had totally evaporated. Now she was not so pliable. Her body had its familiar limits. This was how human bodies should be, right? A constancy of flesh? She watched the woman suds herself, such a massive human. Pubic hair spread sparse and repulsively over her lower abdomen. Her giant brown nipples were like the tips of baby bottles on her huge breasts, those pendulous and implausibly round things. Then the baby in her giant belly turned, and its limbs punched at the surface of skin. And that Adele could remember – the sense of otherness trapped inside, that profoundly and alien otherness that a woman can contain. Then a human emerges, and it, too, is bewildering and strange.

Sometimes Tuuli would say phonemes. Ba. Da. It was a fluke of communication. Usually it was just the screaming, these slices of sound. But when she blurted "ba," Adele would become exaggeratedly cheerful, as if Tuuli had just tuned into the programme of human conversation. The centre of Adele's chest became a conduit of air and hope and velocity.

Adele would try to coax out of her, in a sing-song-y voice, in a baby voice, more words. Not words, sounds, but still. As if Tuuli hadn't been paying attention before, but now she was. Anyway, it never worked. Tuuli retreated back into silence and that luminous half grin, and Adele was left to wonder if she had misheard, if it had really happened. Things could be one thing, or they could be grains of infinity.

That night of the pregnant woman in the shower, it was winter outside, and it was not late, not even six, and there were so many layers to put on. Outside, it was already dark, and Tuuli yelled when the cold air hit her face when the automatic doors rushed open, and Adele carried her and the bag of swimming stuff across the parking lot crunchy with snow and cold, cursing at it all. She slammed her head on the edge of the car, hard, as she slipped Tuuli into her car seat and swore. Adele thought about how, despite the beastliness of that woman in the shower, that woman would nonetheless produce a child that was perfect. This made Adele's head throb more thickly with pain. Thoughts wadded themselves with scorn. It made her body heavy to hate so much. The feeling in her limbs was lead.

On her fifth glass of wine, Adele inevitably started talking in a bit of a baby voice. It was something that sort of happened without her meaning to. At the table, the heavy one was talking about being a single mother. She didn't fit in anyway. She was younger and worked as a journalist and was complaining about it. The woman had written an article about the sociopolitics of stay-at-home mothers in Alberta for a national newspaper, but the story had been killed. She was going on about how journalism was a terrible industry, how no one had properly figured out how to monetize the web yet, and print media was collapsing in front of everyone. The pay was not getting better, and the working conditions were getting worse. She hated it, and the precarity of having a kid to support, too. She had spent three months researching the story. Then the newspaper, with the price of oil crashing, decided that a piece investigating the lifestyles of rich women with rich husbands in oil and gas wasn't "sensitive" anymore.

It's not like the truly rich are hurting right now, not the people that I was writing about, she went on. And it's Ontario purporting to be national media while not even trying to transcend its own regional bias. Of course, she added, academia is no better. Her child's father, she explained, had just lost his job as a sessional instructor at the university in philosophy.

At this, Adele had to cut in. Cody is doing just fine, thank you very much, he just got his Canada Research Chair in Clean Energy and Sustainable Mineral Resources renewed. That's a million dollars in grant money but it goes to the running of his lab, it's not like we get to keep that, people don't realize that about the sciences. It's more about the recognition that he's studying something important. Clean energy is the future of resource extraction economies. Adele's voice was soft, immature. There was a little candle at the centre of the table in a tiny glass jar and she cupped her hands around it as she spoke. The restaurant was a dark din in the background. Her voice was so soft. She felt the other mothers straining to listen. That's why he gets the Suncor money and the Syncrude money, too. Because it's something important –

it's about climate change, it matters to the future of the planet. She paused. Maybe your husband should have studied something more important. I mean, everyone knows that going into philosophy is a bad choice if you want to have a job.

The woman looked shocked, maybe a little sad. Her face wilted a bit. Adele was emboldened. I mean, she said, her voice infantile and shrill at the same time, you can't blame anyone but yourself for your bad life decisions.

Adele decided to redo the entire yard. One of her work contacts, a landscape architect, had helped her design a series of garden boxes and a patio for the garden furniture that she'd purchased online. The furniture was a set of Phillipe Starck's ghost chairs, these bulbous things of transparent polycarbonate that had totally captivated her, in the style of thrones for the kings, but clear plastic. This was, she explained to Cody, meant to be a commentary on the Louis XVI armchairs, which were plush and the epitome of antiques, rich. They were meant to be a commentary on the value of material objects, this plastic and see-through version that she wanted for her garden. The ghost chairs were the platonic ideal of a chair, fleshless and see-through. Plastic is the most ephemeral of materials, too, she argued to Cody. They were simply captivating. The ghost of a chair. Cody, who rarely interfered with Adele's projects because he knew better, warned her that the chairs would break, with the children and the outdoors, and particularly since they were plastic, and plastic chairs should not cost over five hundred dollars, over five hundred dollars *each*, he clarified, but they did. Adele glared at him and pointed out that that was kind of the point. Things break.

She chose pink chintz thyme to grow between the concrete squares of the new patio. She imagined a carpet of pink and green and tiles and fragrance. Gardening boxes of various heights and dimensions so she could plant vegetables and flowers.

When the workers arrived to redo the yard, it was May. She sat on the front stoop and waited for them to come on the day that the workers said that they would arrive. Her house was on a walking route, and, in the neighbourhood, there was a woman who had been a doctor, or maybe she still was one, a medical doctor with a specialty in something formidable. Cancer surgery or hearts or brains or something. The morning was a flush of going to school. Scooters and skateboards and bicycles and the lilac bush in the corner of the yard. Then came along this doctor, or former doctor. Adele watched her walk past pushing her daughter in a wheelchair, but not a normal wheelchair, one of those slightly backward-tilting ones. Heavy duty. For years in the neighbourhood, she had seen them walking, always the mother with the daughter. Adele had never spoken to her. The mother was greying – of course she was not elderly, she just didn't dye her hair – and she was becoming hunched over the wheelchair, so that also made her look much older than she probably was.

Which is to say, this mother was immeasurably older than the other mothers in the neighbourhood, and Adele knew she had no friends. You didn't need to say it aloud. The other mothers dyed their hair and spent money on fashionable clothing. They went to barre classes and ate organic food and went for pedicures and facials and didn't work because their husbands earned too much money to have their incomes matter anyway. As such, they had the impeccable bodies that the barre classes promised and that the spa treatments advertised and, most importantly, the ones that the husbands wanted.

Not this woman. Meanwhile, her daughter was gorgeous, exactly mainstream beautiful. Her long blond hair, her thin long limbs, her sharp features. Her beauty was not at all diminished by how her muscles were atrophied and her head lolled to one side. She looked like her mother, too, or how the mother must have been when she was younger. Adele worried about how beautiful she was. It was a plume of discord in the deep of her insides. Tuuli, too, was beautiful, and, the phrase clung ominous in her mind, Adele said this to herself far more often than she should, as if a grey-haired woman pushing her severely disabled unspeaking bombshell of a girl-child around the neighbourhood weren't proof enough of tragedy: What will happen to her? She couldn't defend herself.

When the workers arrived, it was May. Cody had taken Tuuli to the appointments, because he was leaving for field work soon. Every other day was a thunderstorm, and things were in the flourishing bloom. The lilacs were out on the lilac tree, strident and purple, scenting the yard. The crabapple blossoms on the tree next door were ridiculous, in that moment of apple blossoms that is so ostentatious, those blooms that exist for a week and then disappear and then are forgotten. Flagrant and fragrant. An illusion. The whole yard was floral and deciduous and wet. These men wore yellow reflective vests, and Adele saw how they were all so young, university students who had probably just finished the semester and were only doing this as a summer job. They were so young.

Unlined. Cody was around these kids all the time, teaching them. To him this display of youth was nothing. To Adele, it was arresting. All their hair was dirty blond and curly, as if they were genetic replicas of each other, their bodies all tanned, lithe and muscled identically. Jean cut-offs and dusty work boots. She couldn't really tell them apart. They set to work, and while the blooms made the air sweet, the dust from the sawing of the concrete to pieces clung to the humidity. It was that moment of the spring that was elation.

So she watched as these men hammered the earth, packed sand and soil, cut the concrete tiles, and did you know that all watching is lechery, at its heart, watching perfect young bodies cutting and hammering and packing? Movement is perfection. Bodies are perfection. Lechery is perfection. In this sweet bloomful moment of the spring. Fragrant and alive with potential. How they broke pieces of the thyme into little tufts and arranged them in the cracks between the tiles. Movement is life. Soon the tufts would grow into all the spaces. Soon it would cover the ground in a pinkish green carpet except for where the tiles were, and soon it would be a different sort of perfection, a realized perfection, a latter stage of perfection, and that, too, would be wonderful. Adele relished the thought. How ideas took on shape and dimension, existence, and then flourished and took on a life of their own. After a pure eternity of this Adele went inside to pour herself a glass of wine. Then she went back outside to watch, glass in hand, scooting a delicate chair to a good vantage and felt a warm pleasure extend outward. It was rope-like and prehensile, a delicious confection, blissfully synchronized to the sound of hammers knocking against hollow stone.

A Guy Named Guy

Kevin decided to run for office.

He said: Well, I guess it's time for me to dust off my copy of *Atlas Shrugged.*

You know, said Beta, who once had been his girlfriend but now was not, there are other books about politics that you could read.

But Kevin did not want to read other books about politics. The two years of his electrical engineering degree was enough with formal education. More so than schooling, after all, it was life experience that resonated with people. The ten years that he had spent working construction had given him, he thought, a common touch. People like Beta, with her degrees, could not understand.

Imagine, he said, gazing off to the horizon and holding his hand out in front of him, statesmanlike. Beta knew from this that they were not having a conversation anymore but instead embarking on what would be his stump speech. Imagine, he repeated, that your life's passion is painting pictures. You buy the paint, you buy the canvas, you go and paint your masterpiece. No one bothers you at all. You hang your work of art on the wall, and that is that. But (he paused here and peered out to his imagined audience), what if your passion is building houses?

The speech then touched on the stifling absurdity of regulations in place for home construction: the permits, the taxation, et cetera. Then that moved into a complaint about property taxes and, Beta thought but wasn't completely clear, income tax in general. None of that bureaucracy, he repeated, applied to painting portraits. It was unfair. It hampered human creativity and freedom to have so much red tape. Society needed more freedom. Freedom must thrive. The individual must triumph.

Finally, he finished talking.

So, he said, eyes gleaming and back on her, what did you think?

Well, said Beta, unsure of where to start. Have you ever thought – she finally said, carefully – about how houses need to be connected to water lines, sewer lines, and electricity? That's one way they're different from paintings. Does your utopia involve a lot of port-a-potties?

I would much rather pay a monthly fee for a port-a-potty to a business that is doing good in the world than pay property taxes, Kevin said spikily.

This is to say, Kevin and Beta, when they were a couple, were an odd couple. They met when Beta had a show upcoming in an art exhibit at one of the artist-run galleries in town. She had drafted an incredible and implausible proposal which was accepted. Immediately, she realized she was in trouble. The pitch had waxed about the decay of feminine corporeality and the essential unreliableness of female subjectivity. Big words, big ideas. The piece was meant to be a silicone women's torso that inflated and deflated infinitely. Infinitely!

The plan had been to use the belly cast she made when pregnant with her daughter. Beta unearthed the cast in her closet, where it was slowly eroding plaster-of-Paris particles into her sweaters, and figured out, much Googling later, how to make latex casts from the mould. That was the easy part. The flabby shell that perfectly resembled her once-upon-a-time body, however, was a new challenge. She detailed the latex with a complicated chemical concoction to resemble her own body's colours. But she needed it to inflate. That is what the proposal had proposed. It was a problem. She had none of the tools. None of the know-how.

Then a friend had the idea of getting Kevin to assist. He had access to a CNC router through his work, so he helped to make a MDF frame for the latex cast, a hole cut silhouette-like in the board. Then they (read: he) devised a complicated series of fan and exhaust mechanisms so that the torso would inflate slowly for ten minutes, abruptly deflate, and then lie dormant for another ten minutes. Beta stencilled *UNSEX ME NOW* in Helvetica along the top of the board. It was perfect. The red letters dripped a bit, and that made it even more perfect. She was thrilled. She couldn't wait for opening night.

They were good collaborators. Beta had ideas; Kevin could supply solutions.

The romance, however, did not begin until the night of the opening. It was a sweltering mid-summer evening, one of those July nights that are crowded with concerts and K-days and endless parties. Beta brought her daughter, Milda, along. Milda was six. Milda enjoyed these events in part because they were mostly childless parties: people paid attention to her and gave her treats. On the walk from the LRT to the gallery, the two held hands, their skin slippery with sweat. Downtown was really melting. The sun was still nearly overhead, because it was July. The air zinged with the apex of summer.

Beta had seen the other pieces in the show individually, but all together they were really something else. Plus, there were the performances, which were new to her. When they arrived, a choir was singing a rendition of Guillaume Apollinaire's bestiary poems. It was ethereal and disjunctive. It was called *Le bestiaire/bách khoa về quái thú*. The chanting was textural. The composer was a friend of Vietnamese lineage but who had grown up Francophone. Justin. He was also singing. Beta couldn't understand, but she hoped that that was intentional. Beta began a slow circle of the gallery to take in the other art, letting Milda wander about.

After the performance, she found Justin hanging out with Milda on the patio. The evening was becoming one of those that never cools. It was so pleasant. Everything was so pleasant. The sun was gentle amber. She thoroughly praised the event and his work. There was a barbecue set up, and ice coolers full of drinks. She took a sparkling water, which opened with a spritzy hiss.

Ultimately, I wanted it to be, said Justin, a commentary on colonialism. I translated parts of the Apollinaire into Vietnamese, just my part at first, but then the others start singing it, too. Did you notice? By the way: Is this okay? I've been feeding her. She says she's hungry.

He was slicing up an enormous kielbasa on a paper plate. Beta was a vegetarian. She didn't care so much what Milda ate, but, because Milda was with her most of the time, Milda didn't eat much meat, either.

Yeah, maybe half of it, though? I mean, I thought that was what you were doing, with the Vietnamese. It was gorgeous.

Justin laughed. You realize, he said, this is her third sausage?

On cue, Milda grinned cutely, stabbed her plastic fork into another hunk, and crammed it into her mouth.

She eats meat like Fantastic Mr. Fox, observed Beta. Impressive. She leaned over and made Fantastic-Mr.-Fox guzzling sounds, shovelling imaginary handfuls with both hands. Milda laughed, showing off a mouthful of pink, partially unchewed meat.

I wanted to consider the bestiary as a moralizing device, animals as the exotic other, but when overlaid on the history of French colonialism in "Indochina," Justin started to say.

A terrible whizzing sound interrupted him. It was unmissably loud, and Beta quickly realized the source. Her eyes popped big, and she clutched the composer's elbow in her hand. Please, she said, hold that thought. I promise you I will be back.

She did not come back. She rushed to her installation and saw that a hole in the latex torso had torn open. It was a half moon–shaped mouth, near the left hip. Now air wheezed through, persistent and unhappy. The torso drooped from the wall, defeated.

Well, said Beta aloud to no one in particular, I guess this is terminal femininity. Total collapse, right?

She debated for a minute just letting it be part of the performance. That would work, right? But then Kevin came up and convinced her otherwise. It wasn't a hard fix, he insisted.

They rushed out to get the supplies from her apartment. By the end of it, by the time the sculpture was fixed, the gallery was a full party, everyone was toasting the success of everything. It wasn't hard to be sloppy and glad.

For a few months, their relationship sustained itself. Sure, he wasn't her type, but that was during a period of Beta's life when she was floundering about what her type was, exactly. A construction worker living in a dingy walk-up could be, no? Her previous relationship, with her daughter's father, had illustrated to her that a geeky introvert with emotional problems was not her type. Kevin was the opposite. He did not believe in introspection. He was loud and enjoyed yelling at cars and strangers when they got in his way. For Beta, this was somehow invigorating. She would never.

Physically, too, he was unlike. Whereas Beta and her daughter's father (and consequently her daughter) were tall and thin, Kevin was short and, not soft, just stout. They were darker, with messy dark brown curls, and he was fair, with straight blond hair. At first, too, she was impressed by things like his subscription to a daily newspaper. (Who did that anymore? It was so retro! she marvelled to herself.) They also had mutual friends, punk musicians and vegans and Marxists, which made the lack of common cultural territory between Kevin and her seem less absolute. Plus, he adored her. He was handy and practical. Things were easier with him around.

Soon, though, she did begin to wonder. Those newspapers, how did he read them so quickly? No one could read that fast at breakfast. He just stood at the table, flipping through, not even sitting down, as he ate buttered toast. Then, one day when they were ordering food at the vegan bar that Beta loved and Kevin loved less, Kevin, passing the menu over, asked her to read it for him.

I, he said, need reading glasses to make out type that small.

But, said Beta, you never wear reading glasses. Wait. Do you even own reading glasses?

Or how one day he told her he was sick of her bad jokes.

Puns are the cheapest form of humour, he told her one day.

As if he had access to a secret supply of expensive humour, thought Beta. As if.

Instead, she retorted: Puns are pins on the map tracing the path from word to world.

Now that Kevin was a politician, however, he needed to start doing politician things. For one, he needed to collect signatures endorsing his candidacy. Before long, he called on Beta to help him. He had already asked everyone he could think of, and he was a lot of signatures short of the minimum required. Maybe she could get some of the other parents at school to sign? Milda was in second grade and still liked to be picked up after class. She could ask the other parents to sign, right? This was a real opportunity.

Beta agreed eventually, but only because it was not endorsing him, only his ability to run for office. Let democracy take care of the rest, she thought. Theirs was a famously left-wing riding. The incumbent was well-regarded and capable. Kevin's candidacy would, if anything, split the right-wing vote. She reluctantly took the clipboard to after-school pickups.

She approached a group of mothers from her daughter's class. They stood under the shade of an elm tree discussing homework assignments. Beta walked up and deftly changed the subject. She said: You're not saying you agree with him, or that you'd ever consider voting for him, just that he should be able to run for office. Let democracy take care of the rest.

Even still, the mothers on the little grassy knoll were immediately appalled. For one, it violated the unspoken edict of never speaking about politics in mommy gatherings. For two, no one was remotely libertarian.

Sorry, not the Libertarian Party, said one. Not ever.

Ha! cried another. I thought you said *Liberal* at first!

One openly lied that because she worked for the government, she wasn't allowed to declare her political affiliations in public. (Well, said Beta, this isn't quite that. You're, you know, not endorsing him. And this isn't *really* public. The other mom shook her face jaggedly, as if about to become enraged, she was a lifetime civil servant, Beta knew this about her, so Beta let it be.)

Later that day, Beta returned the sheet to Kevin with just two more signatures. One of the names was the openly climate-change-denying wife of a public health doctor. (The husband frequently appeared on local TV and radio segments, speaking about vegetables and daily step counts. His cheeks were shiny apple cheeks. Beta had never been able to figure out if the wife was ideological or just ill-informed. Maybe she had a wretched sense of humour?) The other was

Fatima, who had been a government economist in Bangladesh but now worked at Tim Hortons while her husband did his second PhD at the university. Fatima was outrageously smart, but her English was not great. Beta wasn't sure if she was a Canadian citizen yet, either, or even whether that mattered. She suspected that Fatima was largely unfamiliar with this particular camp of right-wing thought, and, well, it didn't really matter in the end, because the point was Fatima clearly agreed that Kevin was only hoping to exercise his democratic right to run for elected office.

You know, said Kevin as she delivered the clipboard of mostly unsigned papers to his walk-up apartment, most girlfriends would agree to be their guy's campaign manager. I'm still – he shuffled through the pages, glanced down at the two that Beta had collected and scowled – over sixty signatures short of a hundred. And you have your master's in political science. You'd be really good at managing my campaign. If you only tried.

Beta did have a master's degree in political science, this was true. But she had studied political theory in relation to aesthetic philosophy, and had taken the maximum number of permitted courses in fine arts. These studies had a vast nothing to do with managing political campaigns. Her thesis was on the class implications of the aesthetic of the English garden. She had drawn on Kant and Locke to show that every act of aesthetic judgement was inherently a statement of political identification. Moreover, while she believed she could elbow grease a lot of things in life, campaign management was not one of them.

I'm not your girlfriend, she said instead, which was also true.

This is to say, disentangling herself from Kevin was proving harder than Beta expected. He called her a lot, always wanting to hang out and do things that were reasonably fun. She had a tough time saying no. Plus, Kevin cried when he was sad. But then he made comments like teachers were altogether overpaid, or women definitely shouldn't work out of the home until their children are in school, as if Beta had not put Milda in daycare, and not speaking to him was easy. In fact, she had mostly perfected this art when the business about running for office came up.

The night Beta met Guy, Kevin had insisted that they meet to discuss his campaign. Beta had the night off parenting and didn't feel like cooking. They went to the vegan bar, and Beta ordered a plate of BBQ "chick'n" wings, which were tasty, but she didn't mind food that tasted a little bit like rubber. Her arm, she miserably observed, was also rubber.

At the bar, Kevin complained, as he always did, that everything had the not-quite-normal taste of soy. He was also sour that Beta wasn't more invested in his campaign. The real problem with you, he declared, more cantankerously than was necessary, is that you don't love freedom.

He dipped a sticky wing into cashew "rawnch" dressing and made a face.

Listen, said Beta, who had heard so much about freedom since Kevin had decided to run for office. I don't even understand what you mean by that. Do you mean freedom *from*, like freedom from strife and encumbrance? Do you mean the freedom *to* do whatever you please? If so, how does that freedom interact with the millions of other thusly unfettered and autonomous freedoms in our society? Are they subject to reasonable limits demonstrably justified in a free and democratic society?

Kevin immediately took on a sullen air. He didn't speak.

Meanwhile, there was a performance of drag kings that night, which they hadn't known about in advance. At once, there was a boom of exciting music, and the show was on. Beta had never seen such a thing. She felt nothing strongly about drag queens, which is to say, they were okay, but she was immediately struck by the spectacle in front of her. Drag *kings* were tremendous. Take the emcee, for instance. He was a stout king in a grey three-piece suit, scuzzy sunglasses, and a deliberately pervy painted-on moustache. He took the stage and started telling jokes.

Is it a man or a woman? A man or a woman? he asked the audience. (A beat.) Liz, the answer is no!

The room barely responded. A spattering of clapping, one cheer. For the eight people out there that got that joke, said the emcee, give yourself a round of applause. For the rest of you, this is going to be a long seven minutes.

Even though they were seated at the bar, territory neutral for not laughing, Kevin groaned. Did you want to get out of here? I'm not sure I can handle this.

Beta shook her head. No, she said, I'm staying. This is great.

Then Guy LaGuy came on. He arrived in a tornado of heavy metal. Dio's "Rainbow in the Dark." Flipping across the stage, a flurry of long ashy hair and face paint. His nipples were little jagged lightning bolts. His cape was a bolt of red. Guy landed in front of the microphone, fist in the air and began lip synching: He was lightning, he was a bolt of freedom. The elements came together in a granularity of this revelation. Freedom was this dazzling, a performance. The audience started pumping fists in the air. The noise and movement were transcendent. When he finished, there was a madness of screaming and applause.

After the performance, Guy came to sit at the bar to watch the rest of the show. Or it was Guy without most of his makeup, someone completely different. Beta was one of the only women sitting alone (Kevin had made his exit promptly and as promised), so they started chatting. It took a minute for Beta to recognize who she was speaking to. Makeup does do magic. Those cheekbones! She found out that Guy's real name was Guyonne, but she had swagger and so often went by Guy off the stage, too.

Beta had this unflappable knack of conversation. She quickly discovered that Guy had come to Alberta on her way to pick fruit in British Columbia five years earlier. Loved Edmonton for the culture, which was entirely the first time that Beta had heard this from someone who had Montréal as a point of reference, but then she found out that Guyonne was from Chicoutimi. Chicoutimi! This was, Beta understood almost immediately, not a place that Guy would ever live again. By day, Guy now worked at the federal government, working as a passport clerk.

Turns out those were good jobs. She was one of those workers who set out the little blue sign indicating that she was bilingual. It wasn't much more than simple administrative work, she confessed, her rural Québecois accent the sort that rings like bells, but she was paid well enough, and had benefits and a pension. The government always needed more native French speakers. You just have to be patient with people.

But that, said Guy, is nothing about my passion. This, she waved her hand towards the stage, where nothing was happening at the moment, though a topless, much less exciting, king had just finished their performance, is what I live for. It is a man's world – drag is still so much built around the male gaze – but I do what I can. The queens have become confections, capitalistic consumables on TV, but the kings are still radicals.

So they talked about that instead, which was more interesting anyway.

When Beta got home to the main floor of the house that she rented for her and Milda, having put Guy's number in her phone and having promised to meet her later that week, it wasn't late. She set to cleaning, unable to stop thinking of Guy, feeling that jangly inner electricity that she always felt after a loud bar show without drinking. After meeting someone new. Cleaning meant addressing the detritus of childhood that consumed space rhizomatically. She collected toys and went through laundry. She took Milda's jacket and emptied the pockets: a series of small stones, the pinkish one that looked like a heart, a little chunk of something that might have been quartz that she had insisted was a diamond. A nub of a crayon. A piece of string. A quarter.

A small, mangled feather. An unwrapped guava hard candy from the vegan restaurant. A roll of love notes.

These love notes. When her daughter had first learned to write, earlier that year, her best friend was Rebecca White. Her only pastime became writing Rebecca White love notes. Confetti of love notes. Stuffed into the heat vents and beneath cushions. Each one read the same: I LOVE YOU REBECCA WHITE. Milda hadn't learned lower case letters yet. Maybe this was not a declaration that warranted subtlety, anyway. Beta set the stack on the table.

She dumped the rocks on the ground by the front door, having previously convinced Milda that rocks preferred to live outside in rock gardens. Milda took strings and tied her favourites to the porch railing so that they wouldn't wander off. Beta threw out the whole wad of love notes, save for one. The gesture felt so brazen as to be cruel. Would Milda remember the magnitude of her affection? That love was the practice of love?

Hours later, Beta surveyed her living quarters. Cleaning was so much effort. Once Beta mentioned to another mother at school that she got cranky sometimes that when it was finally the weekend, and she just wanted to relax and hang out with Milda, it was time to start scrubbing toilets. The other mother looked at her blankly. I mean, Beta went on, doesn't the sheer *futility* of it get you down sometimes?

Um, said the other mother, who had a spotless home, the sort that practically invited friends over by itself, like a feature spread out of *Dwell* magazine. We have cleaners come, so, uh, it's not something that really bothers me.

Then Beta felt stupid.

Love was the practice of love. Throughout the rest of the summer and fall, Beta made a practice of watching Guy's practices and performances. She witnessed the whole process. How the scribbly first draft performance had a rough shape. How Guy developed that kernel. Then, how real audiences swooned to see Guy, flush and alive, deliver. Power was in eliciting desire. Guy was in a man's world. In drag, he held power in a leather gloved fist. He was adored. Beta started to make videos of Guy, which racked up thousands of views online. The task was undoing the primacy of the male gaze. That unlocked desire, a free-flowing thing.

Later Beta ran into Kevin while she was walking with Guyonne and Milda. This was November. Spits of snow were swirling about. They were going from the playground to the coffee shop for hot chocolate. Kevin acted as if Beta's absence at the Libertarian Party watch party, which Beta suspected might have been just Kevin, meant that she hadn't followed the results. This was silly. Of course she had. She streamed the elections from home with Milda. Kevin lost, but that wasn't a surprise to her.

He was glum that he hadn't even received one percent of the vote. He seemed to blame Beta. The joke candidates, the guy running for the Rhinoceros Party, for instance, had drawn in almost the same share of the electorate.

Did you think you had a shot? Beta asked. She was trying to be gentle, but his hubris! Their neighbourhood was a left-wing stronghold. His platform made no sense. It was obvious to everyone from the start.

Well, he said, I thought for sure I'd beat the candidate for the Pirate Party of Canada.

After that, Kevin kept calling and texting. Finally, Beta told Kevin that she had met someone. They weren't getting back together. She thought this would provide him with clarity, a sense of closure. Kevin sobbed over the phone. He cried that he would miss Milda grow up.

Who is it? he asked through tears.

Beta exhaled loudly. Guy. You remember Guy, right?

Kevin did not remember Guy.

After this conversation, Beta learned from others, Kevin got mad. In his spare time, he tallied up how many dollars he had spent on her. The account sheet included every time they had gone for arepas on their way home from the gallery and he had paid. Every trip to the vegan bar. He charged her four hundred dollars an hour for the work he had done on "Unsex Me Now." That was the going rate for engineering work right now. He had helped fix her bicycle once, had brought over his tools, which he billed at the same rate. The prize that she won for the work should have been divided in half and shared equally, so he included that, too. The final number was formidable.

He drank in the places where she had formerly spent time. There, he ran into her friends and told each of them exactly how much money she had stolen from him. Stolen! He added that she'd cheated on him with "some guy," and he suspected he knew which one. A few of these people, mostly the crusty punk vegans who had a constitutional distrust of women anyway, were easily convinced. Kevin approached the girlfriend of the guy under suspicion as Beta's new love interest and announced that her partner (Justin, the composer) was double-timing. The girlfriend, Chandra, was satisfyingly incensed. She assured Kevin that Beta would never show her face in the gallery again.

How good, said Kevin.

Some months later, Chandra ran into Beta at the grocery store, both of them picking through the same second-rate produce. Chandra confessed. It made no sense, she insisted, as if convincing Beta. For one, Justin had been doing a residency at the Banff Centre at the time.

Chandra had a Bettie Page-like haircut, black and thick with those bangs. She'd had this haircut all the time that Beta had known her, in and out of trends to do with bangs. Her allegiance to the look, Beta observed as she compared the organic lemons to the ugly lemons, was something. Anyway, she said, she knew Kevin was saying all sorts of terrible things, so she wasn't surprised. Kevin, Chandra said loudly, gesturing with a triplet of bananas, has an anger problem. He was so furious, telling everyone you had cheated on him with some guy and stolen all that money.

This is when Beta found out how much money she had stolen from Kevin. It was an incredible amount. It shocked her. You cannot, said Beta, propelled by a sentiment that could have transformed equally into laughter or tears, charge someone an hourly rate for being in a relationship with them! I could have charged him four hundred dollars an hour for consulting on his idiot campaign!

He would have owed a lot! agreed Chandra. No one voted for him in the end, did they?

He was beaten both by the Rhinoceros Party candidate and the one for the Pirate Party of Canada. No. Almost no one voted for him.

Ouch, eh?

Did beat the Marxist-Leninist, though. That, I think, was a consolation.

They continued talking through the aisles and then to tills and then walked outside together, clutching their cloth grocery bags. It was February, a Thursday. Monday the temperature without windchill had been minus thirty-seven degrees Celsius. With the windchill, minus fifty-one. Today it was raining. Chandra was catching the bus, so Beta waited with her in the bus shelter. Having finished dishing about Kevin, Chandra had moved on and was talking about one of her upcoming choral performances, something by an emerging composer from Montréal. The work considered the plasticity of listening. It would challenge the musical function of sound.

Without preconceived narratives, what is music? It's almost noise art, but more compelling, said Chandra. You need to come.

While they waited, Beta studied the tree growing in the concrete planter by the bus stop. The soil was crusted with gravelly snow and pressed with cigarette butts. A determined elm punched through the mess of it. She could not believe Kevin. How could he? They weren't even together when she met Guy. When would she reach the end of the flat earth and fall off from the territory of men, she thought.

She imagined what it would be to be a tree. This tree, that tree, any tree. Make like a tree and leaf. *Bid the tree unfix her earth-bound root and leaf.* Leaf, leave. As she pondered this, Beta felt her feet become more moored to the ground, rooting downwards through the concrete pad to the infinity of soil below. The connection exhilarated. Guy was not some guy, she was *her* Guy.

Global warming, commented Chandra. Look at this, she said, holding her hand to catch a stream falling from the roof of the bus shelter in her palm. The sound of wet slurried beneath the plate of speckled gutter ice. The sidewalk glistened wet and promisingly. People think that it's about the planet getting warmer, she said, but really, it's about unpredictable weather patterns.

But, replied Beta, newly energized, a revelation unfurling inside of her like a blossom, every day is a blessing.

Charlie in Canmore

Charlie was the only woman at the press conference for the Norwegian athletes. It was a top-secret affair, or so her editor had told her, which Charlie was only able to attend because of her editor's top-tier connections within the world of World Cup cross-country skiing. The Norwegians, he had explained breathily over the phone, didn't normally *give a shit* about Canadian media. But they were going to let Charlie in. We, he had assured her, had a coup on our hands.

Her editor, whose name was Benjamin, was the harried head of a cross-country skiing magazine that, over the years, had navigated online. Yet he remained a character culled from a 1950s newspaper newsroom drama. He insisted on calling Charlie on the phone whenever he needed her. Then, while complaining about how overworked he was, he windily expounded, on and on, until Charlie forgot the original point of the conversation and suddenly it was forty-five minutes later. For sure she knew this: she had been brought in to cover the western leg of the Ski Tour of Canada, a series of World Cup races scattered across the country. Since the magazine operated on the most shoestring of budgets, Benjamin was only hiring local writers. People who ideally knew about skiing and also about writing. Charlie, whom he found through a friend of a friend, was both. She was hired five minutes into the first of their marathon telephone sessions.

The tour itself was nothing so terribly exciting, just a bunch of ski races. But all the top athletes were there, and she had never seen them race in real life before. So, though the pay was dreadful, even after accounting for the fact Benjamin had promised to expense Charlie's room and exactly the cost of gasoline for her to drive to Canmore, Charlie agreed.

In reality, the conference wasn't that secret, at least it didn't seem so to Charlie. She drove to the hotel where the team was apparently staying, just another place on the main drag of Canmore that was neither particularly fancy nor a complete dive. She walked into the lobby, all beige walls and patterned carpet. Taxidermied ungulates, a requisite feature of Canmore hotels, held their antlers aloft above the gas fireplace. Sheathes of media equipment and winter jackets tangled over pine log sofas.

Upstairs, in a tinier space, the actual press conference was underway, transpiring entirely in Norwegian. The interview was with one of the female athletes – embarrassed, Charlie quickly Googled a name on her phone to make sure that she knew who it was – who was surrounded by a flock of men with black media equipment, cameras, television recorders, tripods, cords. The athlete, tiny, dark-haired, and tanned, was wearing her team uniform, a bank-sponsored toque on her head, and a team Norway buff around her neck. All the logos were there. The media men, pressed close around her, kept erupting in chuckles. It wasn't pandering laughter. The woman had awesome comedic timing. Even without knowing what she was saying, Charlie couldn't look away from her gestures and delivery – she was at first nonchalant, then earnest, impressed, then entertained. It was captivating. She leaned forward as if to tell a secret, then broke into laughter herself. She wielded this flirtation with the men, the charm of being just a little bit uncomfortable. The men loved it. Charlie loved it.

Then it was over. Men with black cameras descended from the loft, this herd of Norwegian television journalists, these men who were extras from a Bergman film. The old bald one with bad teeth showing through his laughter. The tall one with the receding hairline and plastic-framed glasses. The younger, blondest one, who had been recording audio on his cell phone. It was a mess of men, and as they descended the pine log staircase, chattering and ebullient, Charlie realized that she hadn't asked anything. She had forgotten what her editor had insisted, that it was okay for her to be asking questions in English. Everyone spoke English, so it was fine. He had even confirmed this with the person responsible for media relations. Oops. The men, the jokes, the Norwegian, showing up late, the charm of the spectacle, it had all distracted her. She fumbled for her phone, which she hadn't even pulled from her shoulder bag, and tapped open the voice recorder. Ready.

For now, though, everyone was waiting for the men athletes. The superstars. The two on the Norwegian team who had the famous rivalry. The two that won the races. The smaller, blonder one, had the incredible stamina and the beautiful technique that Charlie sometimes slomo'd on YouTube just to try to figure out. He was elegant and efficient and strong and had sweetly sportsmanlike behaviour that the television commentators never failed to comment on.

After the races that he so frequently dominated, his blond beard neatly trimmed, his hairline nicely hidden beneath a team toque, after these races he almost always fantastically dominated, he smiled toothily. He spoke humbly, even though it was no contest most of the time, he just took space from the beginning and then kept it for ten, thirty, fifty kilometres. This perfect human metronome of skiing technique. The distance between him and the rest of the suffering and mortal pack growing and growing until the camera could not contain them in the same frame, or even in the same narrative of the race. It was just him, on the snowy expanse of trails, a muscled ideal in motion, crushing not just the competition but the idea that a competition could even exist between him and his rivals. Afterwards, he smiled toothily but so sweetly, so earnestly, and said such complimentary things about the course and the waxing techs after the races. It was impossible not to cheer for him. To believe that he simply occupied a different realm of human physical achievement and fortune. Even when things didn't go his way, even when it was *not his day at the races* (as the television men chirped in their British accents), he never ever complained or blamed anyone but himself. With this etching of vulnerability, the fact that sometimes he lost, that sometimes he looked tired and came in fourth instead of first, his mythology was secure.

Sometimes at the end of the races he appeared on screen with his brunette wife, with their adorable little son, who looked just like him, who waved a little Norwegian flag. You could not not cheer for him.

The other was his Shakespearean foil, darker, taller, with sharper features. A scraggly half beard. He was, for whatever reason (perhaps because he was single, abundantly single), the real celebrity in Scandinavia. A CBC story had come out when the Tour was in Montréal, in which he said he appreciated his ability to walk the streets incognito there, because, he said, he couldn't do that in very many places anymore. Such a heartthrob. His flip of French footballer hair. And he was fast. He could race the short races faster than almost anyone. Certainly faster than his blond rival. But when he skied, and when he skied fast, he had the wildest technique. He was a pure beast, his arms not quite flailing, his body not quite a betrayal. When he raised his hands to pole it was a frantic gesture towards the heavens, a manic praise upwards, his feet locked to the earth and to the skis sliding forward. It was a horrifying, desperate series of movements that screamed about human frailty. Yet this ugliness worked. He was so fast.

And while Charlie watched the blond to understand perfection, she succumbed to the essential eroticism of the dark-haired sprinter. How frenetic and praiseful the motions were, and repeating, his hands up in the air, towards the sky, his legs shooting forward as his poles hit the ground, and his torso, rippled with muscles beneath his race suit – Charlie had also seen the photos of him shirtless on Instagram posing against backdrops of snow and women – this hopeless vehicle of torque and muscle. He skied like a broken man, one who could never do right or be quite right and triumphing despite himself. Because glory was in not wanting any sort of abstract perfection but instead only simple victory, sweet and fleeting. Charlie relished the ugliness of his spectacle, its allusion to hopelessness. The lust, combined with pity, with admiration. He was, after all, a man whose fame proceeded him. He could rarely walk the streets without being recognized.

While Charlie waited, she slumped against the wall of the hotel and checked her phone for emails. Men in front of her rearranged the furniture and lighting. Soon two fake leather chairs sat beneath the warm and expertly adjusted lighting, one chair slightly larger than the other. Charlie wondered, idly, how the skiers would decide who sat where. Whether the smaller man would take the smaller chair without question.

A bustle began again, and what first struck Charlie was their tininess. The dark-haired one arrived in crisp blue jeans and looked very chic and Nordic, while the blond was in tattered sweatpants and ruined Nike running shoes. The blond took the smaller chair without either hesitating. How human accomplishment changes the scale of bodies, thought Charlie. When you see them on television all the time, you think of them as being big. The cameras are so close, and the men fill the screen. It's all you can see. But then the actual bodies are only human.

Again, everything was in Norwegian, with its frustratingly almost-familiar words. Charlie half-believed that if she just listened harder, she could understand, but this was not true. The taller of the two, who sat in the bigger chair, fidgeted in front of the camera and wouldn't make eye contact. Charlie wondered if he was shy. Maybe he was one of those athletes who is secretly dyslexic or always did badly in school. She then recalled the phone in her hand, which had been recording the interview in Norwegian. Right. She was supposed to be conducting an interview.

She waited attentively for a lull, and then, her heart thrumming loudly, she leapt to a stumbling of meek questions in English. How did the Ski Tour of Canada compare to Europe's Tour de Ski? What was the snow like here in comparison? The crowds? The blond looked towards her and smiled brilliantly, his toothy smile, and answered exactly the polite answer that would make a good pull quote for the skiing website. Then it was more Norwegian and more laughter and exposition, and then it was over. The allotted ten minutes was up, as easily as that. There was a gesture from the team manager, and promptly the athletes got up to leave.

Charlie was standing by a pillar when the dark-haired man, on his way out, nearly smacked into her. Then it was easy to talk to him. She pivoted her hips. He curled his body down in the way that taller men do to talk to women who are not as tall as they are. She held up phone closer to his mouth and asked him questions. What was it like to wander the streets of Canmore unrecognized? He spoke, and his eyes gleamed teal. He said something rough, something approving, something not quite a postcard sentiment. How is the quality of the snow? His response was a small spark of exhilaration. The line of his jaw. How were the courses in comparison to the European circuit? Then Charlie's mouth dried up, and there was a crush of people anyway, so he nodded and moved along.

During this time, her children were downstairs in the lobby playing on their iPads. Charlie had planned the trip with them before Benjamin's flustering call came in. She hadn't told him about her children. She knew his response would have been theatrical, outrage and sarcasm and insult. He would have chomped at his imaginary newspaper man-cigar and yelled about how she compromised her professionalism. In fact, what professionalism did she have in the first place? Pre-emptively, she had hinted that she would have friends and family in town who were spectating with her. She was in fact referring to her mop-haired children, eight and ten years old. A boy and a girl. The two hardly noticed her when she came back down. It was just the three of them, all the time. A small family. The dark-haired sprinter was now sitting on a bench by the hotel's front desk posing for photographs. His hair was tussled in a magazine-model way. There was a silver reflective disc angled to his face, directing all the light to him to bathe in.

Charlie walked past him, and, as the camera clicked exposures, her children stepped in double time behind her. The mess of media men was slowly migrating, too, piecemeal, back to the media centre at the Nordic centre. That was a gala ballroom-like room that overlooked the mountains in the Bow Valley. Journos sat at long tables covered by white tablecloths. There was very strong coffee and pastries and fruit in the morning, stew and bread and butter for lunch, followed by little cupcakes, thick with buttery icing for dessert. In the afternoon, an assortment of single-serving bags of potato chips in a giant glass bowl, which emptied almost immediately to contain only the ketchup-flavoured ones. Take some for the kids, the media centre coordinator told Charlie eagerly, he who had politely asked her not to allow the children in on the race days, because the men needed to be able to concentrate on filing their stories. She had, obediently, slipped three packages into her computer bag. He smiled and nodded his head. He was a good guy. A good-enough guy. His girlfriend was from Edmonton, and Charlie knew her, so he was deliberately trying to be nice. His girlfriend was a former World Cup racer herself.

The journo men resumed their places, exactly where they had been seated before. This was not accidental. Whenever they left their spots, they wrote their names on the back of old results pages and positioned them exactly where their laptops had been.

In the front of the room, the press conferences took place. An orange wall patterned with the logos of all the ski tour sponsors served as background. The sponsor names were forgettable. The only one that Charlie could name while not standing there was Le Gruyère. This was because the Gruyère people were distributing little cubes of cheese in front of a tent outside. Ten dollars got you a whole slab of the stuff, and it came with a free Le Gruyère cheese-logo'd skiing toque. It was good cheese. The kids, snacking on the samples, had begged for a full block, and when they brought the money to the tent themselves, the Gruyère people were charmed and gave them two toques instead of one. They also cut open the plastic wrapping, so that when the children reappeared, newly toqued and cheerful, the block had already been half-gnawed down.

Upon their return from the press conference, the media centre guy seemed to forget his rule about the children, instructed her to leave them alone to play at the white-table-clothed tables. He wanted her to get some interviews with the Canadian athletes. Charlie considered the children.

They had already poured water on to the fabric and, with wriggling tongues, were eating whipped butter straight from the plastic serving packages. Tiny coffee creamer cups were arranged as a tea party. Charlie, feeling helpless, told them to *be good* while she was gone.

The media liaison then led her on a serpentine path through trailers and snow and parking lots. Charlie gawked at the thousands of dollars of top-of-the-line skis and poles just leaning, unsupervised, against the outside of the trailer wax rooms. In one of the Team Canada trailers, she ran into a wax tech friend. He had been testing skis for the national team.

Offhandedly, Charlie asked him what the secret was to the glide waxing, what they were doing about the fact that the snow in the shadows was so cold and the snow in the sun just slush. But the formulas were so secret that even he didn't know. He, he confessed, just ran the skis and reported back. I'm not, he joked, any brains of any operation. She told him about interviewing the Norwegians. He laughed and told her that the dark-haired one was on Tinder, right now, available in Canmore. *Right now.*

Charlie's thoughts flitted to her children, how they had probably, at that moment, moved onto to pilfered cupcakes.

Anyway, the interviews were terrible – she was led to a handful of back-of-the-pack Canadian racers. She knew nothing about them and stuttered out bad, embarrassingly vague questions. In response, however, the athletes were uniformly charming. Their optimistic smiles and sunshine-y work ethic made her feel guilty for her lack of preparation. Benjamin had told her to focus on interviewing the international athletes!

After a few of these lacklustre conversations, Charlie made an excuse to slip away. The media centre guy, by day a journalist in Canmore at the local paper, having supervised the awkward exchanges, led her back with no indication of judgement. Cheerfully navigating the ski trailers back to the media centre, he instead chatted about mutual acquaintances in Edmonton.

The next day was race day. It was bright and blinding morning. Spring was early. The air was already warm, well above freezing. The women went first, when the snow was freshly groomed and chilled from the night before. Fast. Conditions weren't going to stay like this for long, everyone said. Some of the racers cut the sleeves off their race suits. They'd get new ones next season.

The racers assembled in the starting area. Those who had been cumulatively faster in the previous races of the series started first, while the others pursued them. The Norwegian women went out the gates before anyone else. First, the tiny blond who won all the time. Then, the dark-haired one Charlie had seen in the press conference earlier. Charlie climbed partway up the first hill with the kids in tow, watching the women pass by. She had never done this before. As with the men, Charlie observed, the women were tinier in real life. Their bodies were like the bodies that you would see every day. Unremarkable. The televisions and the watching of them made them seem bigger. But then, they were also buoyed by the substance of victory, its sweetness and gloss and camera angles.

And yet, unlike when watching on her laptop at home, she could watch the field flit by. It was just a glimpse of the race, a slice of the action. Muybridge-esque. The Norwegian women, the handful of other nationalities at the front of the pack, were all exacting skiers. There was a precision, a perfection, in their movements. This was followed by a slow devolution – the women became less refined, slower, more strained, less elite in their movements. This didn't happen with the men. Towards the back of the pack, a woman in a Bulgarian race suit bobbed side to side as she laboured up the hill, her face twisted and her breathing a wheeze. Charlie looked away towards the mountains, pulling up the collar of her puffy jacket. The wind was more biting than she had expected, especially because they were exposed and higher up on the mountain. Colder than the brightness of the sun suggested. The children had found a snowbank where other children were also climbing up and sliding down. They weren't watching the skiing at all.

Over lunch, Charlie stole paper bowls of stew and buttered bread from the media centre and left the kids in the chalet of the Nordic centre to eat. She went out to ski on the deteriorating tracks. The grooming overnight when the world froze was fabulous, transforming the snow into immaculate corduroy trails. But by noon, it was nearly quicksand. She slipped on her skis to go up the mountain, to the meadow. Her breath panted, and her skis moved slowly on the slush. She saw some men warming up for their race, accompanied by local junior racers. Some of the wax techs were still out testing skis. None of them went as far as the meadows, where the sky opened up blue and vast, and the view of the mountains was sublime.

Soon, she collected children from the chalet, and they went to watch the men's race. In the crowds, Charlie recognized some of the families that surrounded them, some of whom had driven down for the day for the finale and others who had come for the whole weekend. It felt lonely. There, the pomp and the flags and the announcers in both official languages, the sunshine and melting snow, the swirling space of breeze, all moved around this granularity of her family. The single mother with her two children in tow. These children wore the giveaway sunglasses from the expo and, when the skiers passed by, clanged tiny giveaway cowbells fervently. They wore their new Le Gruyère toques and clung to the edges of the fence to get a better view. Then her son, who would curl with her on the couch at home and watch the races with her on her laptop screen, leaned over to whisper that the sun was too bright, and the noise was too loud. It was too much. She let him go play in the snowbanks.

Once the men were finishing their pursuit race, Benjamin had told her she should go to the mix area, a special alley that was marked off with a ropey knit fence, where Charlie was supposed to be "mixing" with the athletes. Really it was for the television journalists, anonymous snowsuit men behind huge cameras, and photographers, who wandered around in stretchy orange vests with PHOTO written in white lettering across their chests. But she went anyway, leaving the kids behind the fence – a pack of children had formed, luging down snowbanks near the ice rink – because the security guards wouldn't let them pass without media badges.

So Charlie stumbled through, in the blinding sun, too shy to speak to the athletes, unsure what to say anyway.

Although she had a sense for the race while watching in the stadium, all she could do from the finish line was to count them crossing the finish line. She had no feed for the results. Because it was also a pursuit race, Charlie had no idea how, individually, anyone had placed. She clung to the net fence between the finishing area and where the media was allowed to stand, watching the athletes flit in and promptly change out of their race suits. The French team was standing right in front of her, and Charlie spoke French, so mumbled to one of them whether he had had a good race and he said, *Bien sûr, c'était excellent.*

After that blunt exchange, another journo, who was France-French and obviously chummy with his nation's skiers, leaned over to get his attention, calling out to him: *Momo! Bien fait!* And Momo leaned over and grinned at him – it was all jubilance, the French corner here, the men half-stripped and embracing – his reddish stubbled chin broad and happy. Charlie felt foolish, after, to see he had beaten out all the others, with the fastest split of the day. Then, he was on the top step of podium, his fists punching the air. His name was even so victorious, Maurice Magnificat.

And more men came in. How in clusters they peeled off their race suits, made a routine of it, unzippering from the neck to waist, pulling out their arms, showing musculature and the undulation of broad shoulders and skin to the sun. Imagine Degas's ballerinas, but men and not ballerinas. That easy, outstretching physicality. The lines of body hewn to purpose. Charlie recognized some of these bodies from the television coverage of the tour, the parts she had watched of it before it had come to Canmore. They had names: Richard

Jouve, Renaud Jay, Baptiste Gros. Their skin was so illuminated in the sunshine.

A woman from Edmonton, the girlfriend of a wax tech for the Australian team, came up beside her by the mesh fence. She was volunteering to give out awards, and she was getting ready to give out the globes or whatever they were receiving for winning. Medals maybe and flowers and these giant slabs of cheese. The cheese was Le Gruyère, naturally, a four-kilogram wedge. This was a clout of cheese. Sometimes the women dropped them by accident, because they were given their wedge once they were already juggling the flowers and the medals and the trophies in their hands. This woman from Edmonton wore a red ski tour toque layered under a trucker hat and stood for a while to watch the men with Charlie. Charlie took her photo, with the mountains in the background. It was a scenic day, with the vast blue of the sky and the brilliant white snow. The photo turned out well. The hats worn together did look funny.

Charlie looked back at the children, now pressed against the blue netting fence that separated the spectators from the media area, crushed against the other kids who also had dull-nibbed Sharpies and were begging for race bibs and signatures.

They look so much like you, your kids, commented the girlfriend of the wax tech.

This is something people were always saying about Charlie's children, because they were rarely seen with their father. So people saw the hair, wild messy curls, and thought it must be from Charlie, who had the same hair, but it was from their dad, too. Then, Charlie's phone buzzed. A friend in

Edmonton was texting to say that she had seen Charlie on the television coverage. Charlie had forgotten that the cameras were projecting out into the world. The experience wasn't at all invisible or fleeting. In fact, this was also her purpose.

And soon after, when the podium was being filled with these men, these fists punching in the air, holding bouquets of flowers aloft, Charlie wandered over, and there was her son, so little through the net fence and crushed against all these people. I'm feeling overwhelmed, he said. He said it so sweetly, his big eyes brown and worried. The crowd was thick behind him.

She went to stand closer to him, near the fence, wrapping her arms around his shoulders, and then Charlie looked up to see the skier who she had interviewed earlier being interviewed by Norwegian media right in front of her. She caught his glance at first by accident, and then he kept looking away from the camera, past the man who was interviewing him, at her. It took her a moment to realize. They were staring at each other. She was standing so close to him. He seemed older, more vulnerable now, crinkles under his eyes, and the way that he was speaking sounded immeasurably more serious, his stubble and his forehead drifting back on either side of his hairline. She could imagine how he would look when he was an old man. His jawline, unshaven, looked a little haggard, and his posture bent over towards the much shorter interviewer suggested, now, less a flirtation than a progression to age. Nonetheless, she felt a surge of endearment, witnessing this vulnerability. He was gesturing and moving and answering questions and looking right at Charlie with a magical intensity.

His team manager rushed up, a woman carrying around a bag of yellow clothes, and Charlie realized that they were the winner's bibs. She gave one to him and put a giant can of Red Bull into his hand for the photographs, not for drinking (of course not for drinking), and rushed him away. Then he was on the podium, tall and belonging to this other universe of feat. The accomplishments were being announced in both official languages. Look at how success is an external thing, this stupendous moment of being tall and standing up so high, so much closer to the sky, surrounded by the eyes of television cameras and people. Charlie thought.

With all this distraction going on, Charlie had her son slip under the fence so that she could hold him, though he was eight now and, really, too heavy for her to carry. He clutched her back, clinging to her gratefully, and when she picked him up, his legs dangled nearly down to her knees. Security had stopped them from coming in with her to the media area earlier, but if he was being held, he was just a child, right? Then the national anthems began to play, and everyone took off their toques to show respect.

Later, her daughter counted the signatures that she had collected and the race bib that some back-of-the-pack athlete had given her. There was no name on it, just a number. Eighteen. The athletes, especially the less illustrious ones, seemed to understand about gestures and enthusiasm to children. Her daughter was ecstatic. Later, they went back to the condo and ate organic macaroni and cheese from a package alongside spears of cucumber. Her friends who were the wax techs posted pictures online of the party that happened after the awards ceremony. One of them piggybacked the tiny blond Norwegian woman, the one who won everything. She had won everything, again. On her face was pure drunk glory, mouth open wide and eyes squinted shut. Or it was a performance gasp of pleasure. Charlie couldn't decide. This woman wore the cowboy hat she'd been given on the podium. It looked like quite the party. Later Charlie went to the washroom and found that she was quite unexpectedly bleeding and quite a bit. She thought about this and counted weeks backwards on Sunday afternoons and who she had seen when. She drew conclusions and felt crescendos of emotion that ultimately landed on relief. Later the three of them went walking just behind the condo, where all the snow had melted. They followed the dry dirt trails up to the top of a ridge, where there was a rope swing, where the children swung out above land towards the rocks and the river and then back again.

The Fighting Robots League

September was a spreading open of gold. The Manitoba maple leaves turned against the blue sky full of high-flung tufts of cloud. Sarah took the dog out to the valley and walked the hard-packed trails. Yesterday was her last day of work. Today was vast and autumn. The leaves, crunching and dry, smelled like exhilaration, crisp and ready. The aspens shed leaves so gloriously. These yellow leaves holding the air and then drifting down. The dog tugged at the leash, and she unleashed her into the dog trail. The sunlight was blissful, glittering with pure amber and possibility.

It wasn't long ago that she had started to dream up this plan of starting a business, while walking her dog through this place. The thought was first a glimmer, but it quickly took on mental substance. This thought-mass started rolling dark and ready through her mind, snowball-like, and increasing. Now she was doing it. Today. The process was a marvel, how a thought could become something substantial. Real.

This was the project. It was still a secret. She was starting a business. She was going to be an entrepreneur. A businesswoman. What kind of business? Well, I'm glad you asked. Artisanal dog collars. Think about it, most dog collars are so ugly. That nylon webbing gets so grubby. You should let your dog be their best self. Give him a bowtie. Give her a bow.

With her Kenmore sewing machine, the one that looked like her mother's but that her mother found on Kijiji when she tried to borrow her mother's Kenmore, she had started to make prototypes. The machine was a solid metal thing from the 1980s, and the engine was a solid thrum of steel when you pressed the pedal. She pressed it into the night, after her daughter had gone to bed and before her husband got home in the evenings. That was when she had her idea. Dog collars. She had begun to make them already.

She had started with one for Rapha, their nine-year-old former sled dog, half husky and half greyhound, dappled grey. Rapha looked like a fuzzy greyhound, thin and fast. She was a rescue dog from when Sarah had been living in Fairbanks. All the SPCA dogs were rejected sled dogs in Alaska, and all the rejected sled dogs had been abused. They had been beaten and starved and tethered and kicked when they weren't hauling the sleds. It was always minus thirty in the winter in Fairbanks. Rapha was shimmery silver fur and jittery, a pure flight response. She hated strangers. She ran out every gate left unlatched. Luckily, by the time their daughter was born, Rapha didn't startle quite so easily anymore. She didn't shake, convulse practically, when someone new tried to pet her. Nonetheless, she was never perfectly at ease.

Sarah made her a turquoise bowtie, with white chevron stripes. It was a distinguished look. Everyone at the dog park asked where she had bought it. Sarah told them that she had made it herself. Everyone was impressed.

These dog-park friends were her first customers. Their neighbourhood was full of young couples who owned a dog, first, to test whether they were compatible as future parents.

It's the stage that comes after they move in together. They get married afterward, that's the progression, after they have the dog, and know that they are compatible as future parents. Look how the bowties let the dog look dressy for the wedding.

She made some without the bowties, too, and some with flowers. They worked for more casual events. Or if you cared that your girl dog looked like a girl. Everyone loved them.

This morning, instead of going to work, she rode her bicycle to the fabric store. Marshall's Discount Fabrics. Beneath the train tracks, pigeon shit muck on the sidewalk under the underpass to Marshall's Discount Fabrics. Up the other side, there was the strip mall of dreams: the cannabis shop, the sex toy store, the Tienda Latina, the mattress store. Zingy with transgression, she fumbled with her bike lock but soon she was wandering amongst the bolts of fabric. It was ten a.m. She rubbed her fingers against corduroy, fleece, flannel, sateen, tweeds, feeling textures like joy. It was an electrical charge. Her feet were light on the scuffed linoleum.

Even the dust in the air was bracing. She thought of when she was a child, and her mother had made all her clothes. Her mother worked on her Kenmore in the room next to her and the sisters' bedroom, whirring and clipping in the evenings after they had been put to bed. The metallic slicing sound of scissors on fabric held tightly to tabletop. Sarah's shoulders relaxed to think of that sound. The nostalgia included memories like when the sister next eldest to Sarah, the one with reddish hair and freckles who was mischievous, would hide in the bolts of fabric at the fabric store. To them, their mother was a towering authority with permed brown hair.

When she was being rung through the till, the three of them would scurry away, slipping between bolts.

Generally, their mother was not quick to temper. But it was unpredictable when she did, a scattershot process to a tipping over. And when it happened, they felt such an incredulous exhilaration. They outnumbered her. Sometimes Sarah wonders if her daughter understands this genre of absolute power that children have. Their mother was so tall. She permed her hair seasonally. Her hair wasn't naturally curly, not like the girls' heady mops. She seemed unassailable. The three of them liked to play tricks on her by hiding at the fabric store. Between the bolts of fabric, arranged upright in those circles on the floor on wire frames, there was space where you could slip through and hide in the centre. The air was dusty to breathe. They nestled in there, suppressing riotous laughter in a soft cloth circle.

When she found them, she was so angry.

These were electrifying moments.

Sarah bought metres and metres of fabric. Yards of cotton weave patterned with polka dots and stripes and licensed images of Batman. Thread matching the fabric and interfacing and parachute buckles and D rings. Her backpack was full. Seventy-three dollars and forty-five cents. The bike ride home was heavy and full of sunshine. She was in awe of fall, when the gusts of wind blew so many amber leaves through the air. Confetti leaves and air, and the blue and the yellow and the strike through the heart of light and wonder. Ebullience.

The space between falling leaves, she thought, pedalling harder, is wonder.

She stopped for lunch, one of those bland sandwiches from the Tim Hortons on the way home, but she knew she wouldn't meet anyone she knew there. She ate, then biked home, and unpacked onto the pine kitchen table. She formed an optimistic pyramid of little bundles of cloth wrapped in elastic bands. She found her scissors that she wouldn't let her daughter use to cut paper. Hauled the Kenmore from the closet. It was 12:15. School didn't let out for nearly three hours. She went for it.

Eleven dog collars later, stacked in a precise and multicoloured pile, it was time for after-school pickup. How neatly the day went, there.

Sarah had a husband and a daughter and a job. Or she had had a job. She had been a registered dietician with the government for nearly fifteen years. She had specialized in perinatal nutrition, which meant that she did consultations and planning and workshops and travelled to small towns in Alberta regularly. She knew facts, like a woman's chance of breast cancer is reduced for every year that she breastfeeds up to the sixth year, and then it doesn't matter so much. Or what kind of things were good sources of calcium, how to relieve mastitis, and exactly the importance of B vitamins during gestation.

She hated it. Nutrition was an appealing choice in university for exactly the reasons she had grown to despise it: the predictability, the ease with which she could memorize and recite information back, the shell of authority it provided over those around her. As soon as she could, she opted to take four-fifths of her income so that she could travel every fifth year. The banked income spread out over that extra year that she wasn't working. She could resume her job when she returned. Perks like this made working for the government make sense. The first time that the sabbatical year had come up, she and her husband had gone to Alaska so that he could do his master's degree. The second, they had travelled in South America. That time, their daughter was two years old, and some people looked askance at having such a young child travel internationally. But the thing about travelling with kids in these countries is that people relate to kids, Sarah would say. They're just more family-friendly cultures.

The third time was this year, and she lied to her husband, who had agreed to an administrative promotion at the local technical college where he taught electrical engineering. He had already said that he couldn't take the year without pay as he had the other two times. She lied to him to say that she was going to bank that year for another year. She did not. Instead, she took the sabbatical anyway and started making dog collars.

She had never felt so grateful that they had never actually married, never combined their finances. She had always made plenty of money, and him, too, or they had made enough. But neither of them really worried that much about money or material possessions. The thought of reading each other's bank statements both made them so uncomfortable. Like scrolling through emails or texting history – who did these things? They trusted each other, that they were always tracking towards the same thing.

Her daughter, Olivia, was in second grade. When Sarah got to the elementary school, she found Olivia emptying and refilling her Mary Janes with sand on the edge of the playground. The playground was a localized frenzy. One of her classmates had stolen the classroom's white vinyl erasers and then buried them in the sand inside her metal lunch container. Her mother had discovered the absence. This was a problem. The metal containers were special-ordered from the States. They cost thirty dollars each!

The girl had forgotten, explained Olivia matter-of-factly, where she had buried it. But she just told that to her mom. Actually, she had made a time capsule. She was waiting for the future to happen before she would dig it up again.

They left the excavation efforts (the mother had got someone to run home for a shovel) and walked home together, holding hands. Sarah wore Olivia's tiny backpack on her back. It wasn't heavy, and Olivia hadn't asked.

That was another thing. She had cancelled the after-school care. She had told her husband that her schedule had changed. None of it made sense, when you thought about it, Sarah realized, but she knew that he did not think too much about it.

When Sarah's husband, his name was Matthew, came home from work, Rapha leapt up and bounded towards the front door. Matthew was tall, a cookie-cutter man of a man, broad shoulders and brown hair and brown eyes. He was good-enough looking that sometimes Sarah felt glad that so few women enrolled in digital electronics. Maybe this only accentuated the ping of jealousy she felt when the pimply males occasionally gave way to a female. These women were all the same. They defied gender expectations by caring about things like robots but, all the same, wore flawless makeup and impractically cropped shirts. They worried about their hair and were smart to boot. But Sarah tried not to think much about that. Not about the pub nights he had with his students. Nor the extracurricular events that filled most of his evenings. *Work* events.

He came in with his plaid button-up shirt tucked into his brown corduroy pants and holding an open cardboard box that jangled as he walked. He kneeled to show Olivia the contents of the box. Inside were the beginnings of the semester's final project: the fighting robots league. Each student had to try to create a robot that could successfully battle and disable the other students' robots. Matthew had never tried this before, but he was the expert. He was confident that his robot would beat everyone else's.

Hey, Dad, called out Olivia. What do you call a cardboard crate full of ducks?

Sarah studied the thinning patch of hair at the top of Matthew's head, the spot that was nearly impossible for her to see when he was standing up or sitting next to her.

I don't know, he said after a thoughtful pause.

A box of *quackers*! shrieked Olivia happily.

Ahhhhh, he groaned. He punched her biceps generously. That's a good one. He then took the box and Olivia, the dog skirting at his heels, out to the garage to start tinkering. Sarah, in the kitchen, uneasily chopped carrots into sticks for dinner.

Words brewed on her tongue. She was good at chopping carrot sticks and fell into a rhythm. Aligning the orange cylinders, slicing with an easy wrist, feeling her sharpened knives slide smoothly through root. She wanted to make grand confessions about unhappiness. About the heavy movements of the day, thick and metal-clad against her skin. About the doom sense of dawn, with its grey cast and limp clothes laid out the night before. The daytime of fluorescent lights and pamphlets. She participated. Her job was a matter of motions with her body: here and there, and talking, and advising, and of course and certainly and this and not that but that and sometimes if then. All in a day's work.

She watched with unfocussed eyes the cool dusk settle in the yard. The garage window became a beacon of warm light. Sarah could see the corner of the work bench from where she stood in the kitchen. Idly, she continued to draft mental monologues. But somehow, as she readied the slow-cooker dinner she still prepared the night before, a butternut squash soup with lentils recipe that requested simmering at low heat for eight hours prior to eating, she forgot them. She defrosted cornbread. This recipe used coconut oil and Greek yogurt instead of butter and cheese. She didn't know how to begin.

The past months, she found that she excelled at deceit. Lies rolled off her tongue without effort. It was fabulous. And what was the difference when she spoke the stories aloud, between one that was true and one that was not? They sat around their pine dinner table, the eight-hour-simmered soup in bowls, dunking that whole-grain cornbread into it, crunching on carrot sticks, and Sarah felt her stories become airborne, untethered. They transcended reference to reality, these tales, and became feathery constituents in wondrous untruth. The new dietician who had been such a pain in the ass that everyone immediately hated her. Until they found out that her son was severely disabled and then they understood, or at least gave her enough slack that she didn't become the butt of all the jokes anymore. (Matthew had nodded, the man in a man's world nodding at the woman in the world of women-things where social inclusion was expressed differently, but he understood, or wanted to demonstrate that he could try to.) Or that complicated something-to-do-with-registered-dietician-bureaucracy problem that had at first threatened the even progress of the day, but they had managed to solve at the last minute! (Matthew wandered off to the kitchen mid-tale and returned with a bottle of beer. Don't worry, I'm still listening! he called out, the refrigerator door swinging open.

He sat back down and, cracking off the twist cap top, generously pretended to care. When he was there, he was there. No one could say that that wasn't true about him.)

These stories-from-nothing gained material miraculously. They operated in curious contrast to those more operatic confessions, sung *sotte voce* on repeat in her mind as she cleared the table and set to work on the dishes, and Matthew worked with Olivia on her homework, but which never made it out into the world.

These confabulations. It was as if they coagulated from the dust motes in the brightness of the sunlight streaming in through the living room in the morning, when, after dropping Olivia at school, Sarah returned to the house and put on another pot of coffee. She just sat, half-blinded in those living room sunbeams, and did nothing. She collected stories from the sharpness of cold in those mornings, the whitening of frost that had started to appear on the blades of grass as she walked Olivia to school. Balancing her ten-speed by the seat with one hand, holding Olivia's gloved fingers in the other, her laptop in her backpack and all external pretense of going to work after the drop off. Stories clotted from the edges surrounding her, the jagged absence of comfort everywhere she went. How did these shards lend themselves to substance? But they did, each a little miracle of genesis that held its own in the world. Like the stubborn warmth that grew pink from her chest as she rode her bike through the cold.

One day, she left her child at school, where it was warm and the linoleum had been freshly polished, and she biked in the direction of her old work. The wind bit her face, gnawed through to her fingers thick with mittens in October. By chance, on her old migration route, there was a coffee shop that was largely frequented by university students and professors. It was a laptop place. She locked her bike to the bike lockup, a metal circle speared by an off-kilter bar and the whole thing drilled into sidewalk. She flicked the heavy lock, and went in. She ordered a latte that came with a leaf swirled in the milk foam and a warm pain au chocolat that was crisp on the outside and gooey in the middle. She filled a small mason jar of cold filtered water from a tap located by the sugar and the cream. Navigated carefully to her table. All of this was new and wonderful.

So in a row in the stream of sunshine bleaching each day whiter and angling lower through the café's great glossy windows, Sarah sat with others like her, studious and engrossed in a laptop. She flipped hers open and began creating her e-commerce site for dog collars. The layout was calming, one of the Squarespace options that looked slick and connected to PayPal automatically. She plunked photographs into the appropriate spaces, typed up this and that about her products and her raison d'être. As her fingers moved over the keyboard, she felt productive, well contained by the universe. Sunshine and dust motes and the warm, milky bite of espresso drowned in milk.

She debuted at the Royal Bison, a craft fair held in November. It was a hipster cool place, with bars of soap made from beer and locally designed dresses. Hand-dipped candles and flower vases made from poured concrete. The customers had ironic moustaches and tattoos, wore plaid shirts and high-waisted denim. There, Sarah appreciated how being a business is not an exercise in idealism. It is not slick like the website. It is physical – there are things you have to pick up and move: the tables, the tablecloths, the sign, the product. These actions are not glossy or Instagrammable. She stacked the collars on the table, arranged by size and style and colour. (This went up on Instagram.) She had told her husband that she was going to the baby shower for a coworker. By the end of the day, two-thirds of what she had brought to sell had sold, and she counted that a success. In fact, she was buoyed.

—

Though it was nearly December, the snow still hadn't come. And so it was still autumn, and so robust displays of decay persevered. The mouldering leaves on the ground. The washed-out shades of dead grass. Sarah's new life had settled in. Monday morning, she went for her morning coffee then walked Rapha down by the river valley where the frost clung to the empty branches of trees. Home again, she took the garbage out and went to the workshop she had set up in the basement. It wasn't a beautiful sewing station, in the extra bedroom downstairs that was otherwise storage, with a tiny window up at ground level that sent a bit of light in, but it was somewhere that Matthew never really went. She stored her materials in the same Tupperware boxes that they used for their camping equipment and cross-country ski wax. She had forged habits there. Everything out for the day, everything packed back away when it was time to get her daughter from school. Still, though, it was perfect.

At first, she didn't hear the phone. The landline was upstairs. She had gone up for another cup of coffee and was startled when she heard the ringing. The man on the voice was upset. I'm so sorry, he muttered. What? Your dog. I hit your dog. She ran across the street, so fast, I didn't see her coming at all. I couldn't avoid her, she ran directly into my path and I couldn't avoid her. In my car. I hit her.

In the bleak and even grey light, Sarah ran out into the neighbourhood to where the street was that she had been told about. There, Rapha was a pool of blood and fur and crushed bones. There was a collapse of senses. On the asphalt. Beside the curb. A bent red fender.

The man helped wrap Rapha in old bath towels. Sarah didn't know what to do. He was even more upset when he saw how Sarah was. He wrapped Rapha in old bath towels they fetched from the house and carried her and laid her on garbage bags on the back porch and then Sarah went inside and started drinking. She called a friend to take Olivia home from school and she didn't know how to tell this to Olivia, either. She was at the table, her face red and blotchy, her teeth stained with wine, when Matthew got home.

What is going on? he said in a rush.

Sarah had managed to get a hold of him once his lecture was finished. He had come back immediately. When he first picked up the phone, he had started to tell her about how his robot had actually been defeated, the students had had a Darwinian advantage, playing against each other before the final competition, evolving, while he had only untested inventiveness, but Sarah cut him off with her sobs. He listened as she described what had happened. Carefully, he said he didn't understand how this could have happened, any of it, how Rapha had escaped because the back gate was latched when he left in the morning, he swore it was latched because he was always so careful about making sure the gate was latched, because he knew how quickly and certainly Rapha would bolt if it wasn't. They should have put their cell numbers on her tag ages ago, but how did Sarah get the call at home anyway? She couldn't speak then, she just made noises. When he walked through the door, made his entrance, he too looked crumpled, as if despite his golden life, he, too, had experienced tragedy. Sarah just stared at him, her glossy wet eyes still red with rage and horror at him.

Oh Beautiful World!

Day 1

The hotel room was cheaper than had Phoebe expected. She had expected a cheap room. She had been warned not to expect opulence. But, still. This was pretty cheap. The curtains were a thick burnt orange, stiff with ancient fire retardant. The thin, oily carpet was worn from brown to yellowish beige where innumerable feet had crossed the room. The furniture – just two beds, a television on a stand, and a small table with two chairs – was unbreakable institutional stuff from the eighties. And, although they had been promised a kettle, there wasn't one.

But she thought of herself as a make-lemonade type of person. This will do nicely, she announced loudly to Harold, who, hauling the bigger of their bags into the room, was struggling in from the hall. She slid open the door to the balcony, a narrow platform overlooking the ski resort's parking lot. Beyond that, the maintenance buildings for the resort. Beyond that, the outline of mountains and the setting sun. She exhaled.

Harold carefully placed the luggage on a hard surface and began his routine. He kneeled down and pulled at the sheets, pried at the mattresses, fervently checking the beds for bedbugs. This is what he did when they stayed in places like this, the ones that turned out a little less nice than they had expected. In all the times that Phoebe had observed him perform this drill, he had never found bedbugs, or even evidence of bedbugs, which led her to believe it was more gesture than a true safety precaution. She wondered if he had ever seen a bedbug in real life. Nonetheless, she was grateful. She would never bother. She had never bothered. The mattresses barely budged under his hand as he pushed himself upright. No bedbugs, he announced decisively.

Or none that I could see, at least, he clarified.

Two weeks earlier, a friend of a friend had messaged Phoebe with a plea: a gravel cycling stage race needed more women to pose for marketing photographs. They'd receive free lodging at Panorama, which was a mountain ski resort, and a discount on registration in the event. A free meal on Saturday plus electronic copies of the professional-quality photographs. This was to take place in September, in the shoulder season between downhill mountain biking and downhill skiing, when the resort went latent. Phoebe heard a battle cry, subcategory representation of women in sport. She was impressed that the race organizers would be concerned about these dynamics. Representation matters! Also, she liked free stuff. She said yes. Harold, her boyfriend of five years who was objectively a better cyclist (and also, objectively speaking, a better cynic) agreed to come, too.

In her mind, it would be a nice weekend away. Maybe even romantic. She had never been to Panorama. It sounded beautiful. People she knew visited for a weekend or longer and spoke nonchalantly of it as a casual and affordable luxury. In the winter, they skied and posted photos of bluebird days, brilliant skies and blinding snow. In the summer, they rented downhill mountain bikes and did terrifying runs. Afterwards, they boasted about their bravery. Even the word was beautiful: Pan-o-rah-ma.

Now that they were in a dorm room, obviously intended for single skiers to stay cheaply near the slope, a reverberation of doubt entered her mind. This might not be the weekend she had envisioned.

Well, what did you expect? asked Harold.

Of what?

Of all of this. They weren't ever going to give us the luxury rooms.

The two were cranky. The drive had taken much longer than expected. Traffic. Construction. Congestion. They started off from their city on the prairies. Harold, as the highway crept into the slate-grey and towering mountains, as they inched forwards and amidst other vehicles that contained humans with the same audacity of weekend escape as they had, said: How do you describe mountains anyway? Now dark, now glittering, now reflecting gloom, now lending splendour?

Harold went off like this sometimes.

The thing about sublimity, he continued, is that people use that word as if it's a synonym for vast beauty, something too big to imagine easily. But the Romantic poets got it – it's really about feeling small and terrified in the face of nature's vastness.

But it is also about beauty, replied Phoebe, maybe a little tartly. It's the beauty of that nature that does that to you, not just the terror of it being large and menacing.

Uh huh, said Harold in his tone that meant he didn't agree at all, but he would not bother to disagree.

What about gridlock, Phoebe pondered aloud. Would that then qualify as a different sort of sublimity? By your definition? There's nothing beautiful about gridlock. And cars are a type of nature, subcategory human nature.

Harold stared off at the jagged blueish grey skyline and didn't say anything back. In his silence, Phoebe thought of photographers like Burtynsky and wondered if she was wrong. Is there a sort of awe-ful beauty in civilization's decline?

The truth of it was that Harold didn't like the outdoors, even though he lived his life as an outdoorsy type of person. He was, for instance, afraid of bears even in places where bears didn't live. Nature was safe when it was manicured, predictable, and predator-free. By day, he worked in a safe place. He was a Land Man, negotiating contracts for oil and gas rights. He had done better with his English degree than Phoebe had. Flipped his honour's thesis on "Bartleby, the Scrivener," having ridden bikes semi-professionally throughout his twenties, into a job as a Land Man. This had taken place during one of the booms where everyone was hiring anyone for oil and gas jobs. (Phoebe always capitalized the job in her mind, Land Man. And, as with most jobs earmarked as socially successful, she still only vaguely understood what it entailed. Brokering agreements between landowners and oil and gas companies to take the oil and gas from under the landowner's land, she had explained to her mother, long ago, who had asked but held a similarly militant non-interest in all things related to oil and gas. It was the most unecological of industries; it did not deserve attention. Because landowners only own the surface rights, not the rights to the resources that lurk beneath? Phoebe trailed off with a high rising terminal. Harold, who was there, did not jump to correct Phoebe's description, so she assumed this wasn't wrong.)

At the time, his total lack of experience in anything related to what was required of him didn't matter. They were boom times. Phoebe could swill the memory. And while most of the guys who got ahead at being Land Men were wild, boozing extroverts, the cuneiform of their right-wing politics worn on their sleeves, somehow Harold managed to make a go of it. Despite being much quieter and entirely less conservative, he was accepted. He was quiet, competent, calm. During this particular boom, the most recent one, magazine articles speculated that maybe people like Harold represented the future of the industry. The bicycle-commuting, left-leaning, green energy-inclined yet-nonetheless-an-oil-and-gas-worker worker. These articles plastered over Phoebe's sometimes obvious, sometimes less obvious, guilt about Harold's unenvironmental career. She saw a movement that ultimately arced towards a sustainable future. Or dwindled into some ruins of capitalistic hypocrisy and, in collapsing in on itself, allowed the planet to win. This is how she functioned as an optimist.

Harold instead focussed on the emptiness at the centre of this greenwashed vision. He, for one, didn't feel particularly strongly about oil and gas. Certainly, he did not see it as an industry ripe for redemption. He was not in its cheerful, workerly ranks of transformation. Subterranean mineral rights were the literal opposite of sunshine. Eventually he wanted to do something else, but he didn't know what that would be. What could it be? Maybe that apathy – a dull loyalty to bloated oil and gas incomes, a tastelessness for the ineffable nature of solar and wind power – he sometimes thought this, to himself and aloud, sometimes he was a broken record on this topic – was also the future of the industry. Whistling that tuneless song of carbon sequestering.

On the highway, a Petro-Canada station appeared on the right. It was a landmark. Geographically, because it was near a bedroom community that used the gas station as a car-pooling hub. The gravel service road was invariably lined thick with parked cars. Emotionally, because a washroom break was always required at exactly this point in the trip. Phoebe was devastatingly ready for it. She rushed out of the car.

In the folly of the snack aisle, relieved and considering a bag of ketchup Doritos, Phoebe wondered if Harold was becoming dour. Once last summer, a friend from his university days, who was passing through town, came over to eat takeout on their back porch together. Back in their university days, this might go without saying, Harold was more left. It was hard not to be. All the books. Memoirs of a million different types of minority experience. The casual Marxism of everyone. Queer colleagues coming out as trans to a perplexity of gender theory that was still oriented around performativity. His political drift away from this, an ebb in one direction, year over year, was less ideological than practical. He never felt as if he really had that much choice in the matter. He needed a job. He wasn't qualified for much. Being a specialist in Bartleby the Scrivener hardly helped his CV. It was an erosion of saying no, not a newfound enthusiasm for saying yes. The pillars never changed, about justice and ecology, but how do you *do* that? This friend was hard-scrabbling it with a job at Habitat for Humanity, with three kids under the age of five, a wife who had gone from being a little bit Christian to a lot Christian after they married. After their firstborn, she quit working outside the home and began insisting on things like church. This friend had little patience for Harold's existential moping.

So your job now, he computed, gnawing on banh mi through a revelation, is that you're a swindler?

Harold stopped chewing for a moment. Swindler, he thought, was a bit on the nose. He swallowed too soon and winced as a lump of bread crust scraped his throat.

You can't swindle people out of something they never owned, Harold said with forced lightness. Fee simple land title in Canada hasn't included subterranean natural resources for decades. On a lark last month, he had started growing a beard, reddish brown and tinged with more grey than the last time he had let his face grow. He brushed crumbs from his chin. Critique the philosophical tenets of land ownership that underpin our colonial society, if you like, he said. Take it up with Locke. Take it up with the courts. I didn't make these rules. You own the land, but not the minerals beneath the surface.

But you play by those rules, said the friend. You choose that because you profit from them.

Neither Harold nor Phoebe really knew how to respond. The profit was obvious. They lived in a relatively nice home in a relatively nice neighbourhood in a relatively nice city. (Their friend did not.) They were not rich, but they were comfortable, a sinking-soft state of being. The alternative, they imagined, was a taunting, gaping chasm of despair and need. Extremities of hopelessness. Their friend proved how empty that hyperbolic threat was. He still existed, didn't he?

It is cool, said Phoebe deftly, that this restaurant is doing so well. (It was owned by a friend-of-a-friend's husband.) The branding is punk, but, like, he got his pharmacy degree and threw it away, just decided to start making his grandmother's favourites. It's a commentary on cultural continuity. Very punk, no? Next time, we should eat in and try the phô.

Their friend nodded agreeably and Harold interjected, but do you think I *want* my tax money going to pipelines? Do you think I *want* to be an anti-hero in an epoch of environmental collapse?

Well, said the friend. As Marx pointed out, everything is fundamentally a social relation.

Less controversially, at least by the politics of their English-department cohort, at whose informal, semi-regular reunions was how Phoebe and Harold reconnected years after university, Phoebe taught business writing at the community college. She, a lover of mid-branching sentences, wasn't a good business writer. Her students weren't good business writers, either. Unlike Harold, she felt quite clear about what she wanted to do. Per the oil companies' habit for three letter acronyms, it was what she coined "ABW": anything but business writing. But by the time she realized that she was also a terrible playwright, the price of oil had tanked. She was stuck. The glossy magazines that sang Sybil-like of industry renovation revealed themselves instead as fickle desert flora, blossoming only when drenched in price-per-barrel dollars. A prominent magazine publisher, channelling the economic desperation Phoebe associated with drought-stricken Indian farmers, killed herself. (Shortly before she died, an investigative journalism piece revealed that she had not paid any of her writers for months.) It was horrible drama. So, as the downtown office towers emptied out and businesses left and right collapsed, both she and Harold were cowered back into the base gratitude for having work at all. Economic cycles were tiring, but maybe they simply lacked imagination. Maybe they were just comfortable enough.

They stopped again in Canmore for lunch, at the French bakery that sold delicious half baguette sandwiches. But when Phoebe and Harold arrived, they found the bakery was sold out of their favourite items. The rest of the menu consisted of either elaborate French desserts or loaves of bread. The worker, speaking English with the cartoonish France-French accent of every single other worker who had ever worked there, informed Phoebe as much. (They also would never, ever speak to you in French, as if it was an order from head office: only speak English in that clotted, Madeleine-esque accent. This irritated Phoebe, whose French was better than their English and thus, in the calculus of such things, this should have been the spoken language between them. But that was not the charade.) The worker invited Phoebe to order something else off the menu.

The desserts were off at a distance. Phoebe asked the waitress to name them. She had napped on the car ride and was feeling a bit groggy. She was wearing a mask. She squinted. When she made her selection, she recognized that she was mumbling. A jumble of syllables in her mouth spilled out. A flourless chocolate orange cake had caught her eye. That is what she wanted.

Phoebe received the dessert in a small cardboard box and Harold had ordered a plain baguette because they were there, and they'd eat it eventually. Fifteen kilometres on the highway later, when Phoebe opened the box, she found the wrong dessert.

No, said Harold, that's what you asked for.

No, said Phoebe, I wanted the chocolate orange one. She must have not heard me through my mask. I don't think I was speaking clearly.

No, repeated Harold. That is what you ordered.

The argument occupied the rest of the drive. Its essence was whether Phoebe had the equilibrium of identity to be able to report correctly on what she herself had said.

You keep saying that you have had these dissociative episodes, insisted Harold.

Phoebe recognized in this comment, of course, the height of insult. That only men throughout history could appeal to objectivity, et cetera. The argument had a lot of philosophical momentum pushing it forward. Phoebe helped push it forward, too. She might have been bad at business writing, but she was good at feminist argument.

Now in Panorama, Phoebe was still sour. But, not having left town for months, she had overscheduled their time. This was not a discussion that she had had with Harold. The first of these plans was to run a vertical kilometre on the ski hill. She had done her research online. There were two paths that had nearly one thousand metres of elevation (930 metres, precisely), and she had it in her mind that she could run one after they drove for eight hours to get there. She announced this plan simply. Harold indulged her. He hated running but would do it with her when he felt a certain barometric pressure to do so. Today, after the drive that they had had, was such a day. He put on his running clothes in the bathroom. She put on her running clothes in the main room, the fire-retardant curtains half-closed. Phoebe knew this meant he was still mad at her, but she was also still mad at him. So there. Earlier, she had pulled a glossy pamphlet from the check-in desk that showed some of the trails. She stuffed it into her pocket for a map.

Outside, the sunlight was hot, tremendous, bleaching. On their skin, acrid-heat sweat soaked into oily-car sweat. Phoebe and Harold surveyed their new environment. Up close, this was certainly a mountain: grass, incline, but it was not the nice sort of grass. Not green grass. It was white and yellow grass that was tall and bristling, all sharp edges. Mounds of ugly dirt pocked the mountainside. Ugh, thought Phoebe. The map that she had pilfered was a bad map. They could see some downhill mountain bike paths, but nothing resembled the route that would take them to the summit. Phoebe felt this was all wrong. There was supposed to be something heroic about this experience. There was supposed to be less ugly. This was entitlement, the responsible part of her mind announced. This is just a different type of beauty, she told herself. You, too, can appreciate this. Ugliness and beauty are arbitrary values: one can become the other with the mind's effort. They ran partway up a downhill mountain bike track, whose corners were fortified with arcing plywood ramps, three metres tall. They ran up, they ran down, they still couldn't find the trailhead.

Eventually, Harold called it. He insisted that they consult the map more thoroughly. He knelt down to draw his finger over the spread-open map. Phoebe still felt a combustible rage at being mistaken for someone who was not self-aware. She felt disarmed. This unaesthetic mountain, this inadequate map, this man through whose thatch of hair she could see scalp.

Harold agreed to go down to the front desk to get a better map. When he returned, sweat beading his pinkening cheeks, this was all at an altitude they hadn't experienced for months, he informed Phoebe that most of the trail system was shut because the resort was currently felling trees all over the place. So, he said, wiggling his index finger over the much more detailed depiction of the terrain he now possessed, we can run over here, but not anywhere else. It was good I went down, all said. We don't want to be slammed by a falling tree.

So they did that, and then went back to the room, ate lukewarm lentil salad leftovers on the sun-scorched balcony overlooking that barren white-gravel parking lot, the leftovers wouldn't keep after all, along with torn-off pieces of baguette from the French bakery. Then they went to bed. Just after shifting the depleted pillows to feel, finally, acceptable, Phoebe got up once more to tug the crack between the curtains closed.

Day 2

When Harold talked about cycling, he talked about forgetting. Like, if you were asked to join a bike ride once, and you didn't say yes, maybe you'd be invited again, but not if you said no twice in a row. Even if they were your good friends, even if you had ridden with the group for years. You were forgotten. That is just how it worked. It happened more quickly than you ever expected. That went for the grander trajectories, too: amnesia was everywhere. Racing teams came and went, coaches, bikes, bike mechanics, everything. There and then gone. He had never ridden in a team jersey for a team that he didn't belong to. This included immediately giving away his team kit when he quit racing his pro team. (It was high-quality stuff, Giordana red, and he gave it to a friend who wore it on his cycling commute until the Lycra panels on the bum became embarrassingly transparent.)

This was Harold's way of talking about himself, Phoebe knew, as he reconciled himself to how he was not getting any faster on a bicycle. His best days were behind him. Et cetera. Once, he was on the national team, once he had won all sorts of provincial titles (the only person in their province to have won all three provincial titles in one year: mountain, road, cyclo-cross), had podiumed at nationals more than once, but you cannot ever rest on past laurels. The past is the past. Every day you must prove yourself anew.

Now, in the absence of such exercises of proof for several years now, he claimed, no one knew who he was anymore.

Yet when they met in the morning at the Tim Hortons in town, the cold parking lot and the cusp of daylight grey around them, Harold commanded an immediate respect. The crowd was composed of strangers to Phoebe. But the organizer was visibly happy to meet Harold, in that way that men greet men, and the women are adjunctive. It was something about Harold's jawline, Phoebe knew, or how he held his shoulders in situations like this, that communicated that he was someone to be taken seriously. Some of the others knew Harold by reputation. They were happy that someone of his calibre had decided to come for this weekend. They said as much. Harold, thought Phoebe, not for the first time about this sort of thing, was such a liar. Forgetting isn't necessarily that easy. They saw in how he held his head up that he was to be taken seriously. How he held his chest forward, even as his shoulders curved. This was a man who had spent a lifetime curled over a bicycle.

Half an hour later, they were on their bikes, peering at the trail ahead, which crept towards the sky at a ten percent grade and was littered with baby head scree. Between the boulders, slippery rivulets of sand. Sometimes the lines were obvious to Phoebe. She could grind and try to keep traction. She and Harold had done gravel races before, on hard-packed side roads, but nothing like this. Their tires were too small and their gearing all wrong. Finally, Phoebe slung her bike on her shoulder and started walking. Her breath plumed clouds in the cold morning air.

One of the women, the friend of the friend who had put out the call for more women, groaned when Phoebe complained about not having switched out her tires for something wider. They were cyclo-cross legal, too skinny. Scoff. This woman had completed races like the Dirty Kanza (isn't that name racist? asked Phoebe), which was what real gravel racing was about.

It's named 'dirty' for the gravel roads and the dirt you get on your legs and body when you ride them and 'Kanza' for the state, which gets its name from the Kaw tribe, she said, matter-of-factly. Anyway, she said smoothly, lathering on effect for the next word: *adventure*. It's *adventure* racing. You haven't done anything that is real gravel racing. Those aren't *adventure* tires.

Okay, said Phoebe, who wasn't feeling very adventurous anyway.

They made for a nondescript crew, this dozen-or-so cyclists with mid-range-or-better bicycles and fitter-than-average body types. They had been asked not to wear their team kit, unless it was the event's kit, which no one owned, save for the guy who appointed himself as the group leader. He had purchased it at last year's event. Harold knew some of these people, because everyone still kind of knew Harold, from his racing days. But he didn't know this guy, who soon revealed he was a professor of engineering at one of the universities. With a scruffy beard and an athletic beer belly, the inability to stop talking about himself, he was a type.

Last year, he explained, he rode with his buddy for the first four days of the tour. But on the last day of the tour, his buddy threw in the towel, and so he rode by himself and could really rip. He finished seventh! On that leg!

This guy insisted on riding first wheel, even though he wasn't fastest and certainly didn't know the route. (Last year, he panted, the course was completely different!) At each intersection, they had to wait for the tour organizer on his pedal-assist mountain bike to catch up. The photographer was even worse, riding a sturdier e-bike that resembled a small motorcycle, all the while gasping and taking corners too fast. His skin was chalky, his face a mottled, corpse-like grey. How, thought Phoebe, was he even alive? Meanwhile, professor droned on. No one interrupted his steady stream of tips and tricks to ride this sort of terrain. The thing is, the best line isn't always the obvious line, he intoned. Phoebe, endeavouring to emulate the tact of her peers, bit her tongue.

Periodically, they stopped for the photographs that were the purpose of the whole expedition. A very dull exercise. They stood around while the drone got into the air, or the photographer hid behind a tree to angle towards where the path was illuminated most beneficently by sunshine filtered through the tree cover. Next, they rode this section of terrain, completely cold and shivering, and tried to make it look as if they were warm and mid-race, but jovially. Just remember, reminded the race organizer cheerfully, clapping his thick gloves together, the race will take place in July!

In one of these lulls, Phoebe started chatting to a man in the group she didn't know at all. He looked much older than he was, but his facial hair was distracting. A soul patch. Phoebe hadn't seen a soul patch since forever, excepting on the sort of guy that, she could say, had an obviously antecedent heyday. But this guy must have been in his thirties. He was perplexingly attractive. Women had so many categories of a repulsiveness that turns out to be attractive. But for men? The list seemed much shorter: the decrepitly old but obscenely wealthy man. Or maybe also, the slightly racist but very wealthy man. For men, it was more about money than appearances. But this, she thought.

It turned out he was from South Africa. Pretoria.

Oscar Pistorius lives in Pretoria, Phoebe noted quickly.

Nah, he said, in a dulcet South African accent. Oscar Pistorius lives in a jail.

This was one of the things that Phoebe was good at, random facts about random places. In addition to Oscar Pistorius, Phoebe had just copyedited an article about South African land redistribution and constitution reform. She mentioned that in the same way that she generally sought to tell people from elsewhere that she knew something about their places of origin, as she had with Oscar Pistorius, as an offhand remark. (She didn't mention that the article had argued that the constitutional reform was essential for South African society to move on from its apartheid past. It was justice, in the country's newly recognized twelve official languages.) He, who had been lounging sideways against the top tube of his bicycle, however, stood up straight. What was happening in South Africa was devastating, he began in a rush. Here are the companies that are leaving South Africa, right now. (He listed many companies similar in size, large, with internationally recognizable branding.) It represented a colossal flight of capital. There are no economic opportunities left in South Africa. This is why he had chosen to come to Canada.

His name was Guy.

Later they came across a giant tree that had fallen across the single track. The vegetation and soil around the log on the path made for a decent run-up. Norm, the flashy young cyclo-cross talent who was there for heavens knows what reason, decided to ride it. The photog got a good angle on the feature and got ready. Norm gave himself a good ride-in and then arced his bicycle cleanly over, gazelle-like and nimble. The finesse! The photog was happy with his snapshots, and the rest of them were impressed. They applauded and cheered as if he had won something. Hooray! This attention, however, meant that the professor of course had to, too. He insisted that the photographer resume his position, crouched down in the moss and ready. But the prof yanked his front wheel too late, messing it up, and instead of sending himself gracefully over, bucked himself into the ground. He landed, ignobly, smearing his face against a bed of moss and knocking his helmet on a root.

Phoebe smothered a smile in her filthy, full-fingered gloved hands. Slapstick was also a form of justice. Norm and Harold rushed over to see if he was okay.

The pass was called Tegart Pass. The namesake was colonial. The Tegart brothers, Walter and Arthur H., first cut a pass to the Kootenay River in the 1880s. The race director noted, however, that it had been used as an Indigenous route for centuries previous. Phoebe wasn't sure if this was true or just something he said. I mean, it was true everywhere. That the Indigenous had been there first. No research was required. It was a statement unbothered by actual land acknowledgement. That said, to her, this route didn't seem like anything someone familiar with the land would pick. It snaked vertically to dense trees and continued its senseless ascent through those forests before flattening out for a bit. On the other side, she could see that the road (gravel! they could have ridden it without hypocrisy!) they had taken this morning to the trailhead had sensibly continued to the other side, without this unnecessary, straight-up-and-down detour. A million photographs later, they launched themselves down these descents brazenly. On the preposterous switchbacks, her too-skinny tires dug deep into the loam.

In the evening, showered, sore, they walked to the golf course for the promised free dinner. After their day, Phoebe and Harold had taken to talking admiringly about calories. Imagine French fries with mayonnaise. Fried eggs. Tacos. Shepherd's pie but made with lentils instead of ground beef. What about a milkshake for dessert? This occupied their conversation for the walk over to the golf course's restaurant while not just their stomachs but their whole bodies ached for food. It was a soothing conversation. Their minds contained cornucopias.

They arrived at the same time as the photographer and the race organizer. At first, they were seated at a table in the grand dining hall. Their server was a twitchy man who seemed impossibly old to be still serving, in his forties at least. He had decisively aged out of being cutely servile, Phoebe observed, with his neck tattoos and hand tattoos and a distracting fidget as he recited the day's specials. His ashtray voice exhaled fatigue. Just look at how impassively he passed out the menus.

In the restaurant, the ceilings in the hall were grandiose. Windows all the way up that high, framing the mountains. The tables were the requisite distance apart and at each, a throng of homogeneously pinky-white drunk men wearing polo shirts were being exuberant together. The experience was dazzling and terrifying. Phoebe would say that she couldn't remember being in a room with so many white men, but then Harold would point out that she hadn't been in a room with hardly anyone for months upon months. It wasn't just the white men. But the mood was solidly a varietal of frat party. Beer bellies stretched out those pastel-coloured polos. God was alive, magic was afoot. The air was a froth like pale lager.

Harold was more immune. These were also his people, although they were not his people, that was the point of at least part of his existential angst. He was inoculated from it. He did, however, want to sit outside on the patio. The race director and the photographer, whose simultaneous arrival meant that they were assigned the same table, agreed.

Outside was better. The patio was huge, curling around the entire exterior of the restaurant, with dozens of tables covered by umbrellas. Some plastic couches arranged around small gas-burning fires. They found a space. The new seating allowed a better view of the golf course, a curving green and manicured vision. Immediately, they discovered the comedy of late-in-the-day golfers trickling in from the last of the eighteen holes. It was fantastic slapstick. Little mobile units went out to feed them more drinks. The golfers' thirst was powerful; their golfing precision was not. At this point, it was a Three Stooges routine, and Phoebe and Harold had great seats for it. The two began to chuckle and laugh, and the feeling began to roll in on itself, become crescendo-y and profoundly nonsensical. They were too tired, they hadn't eaten enough, their day had been spent climbing craggy angles this golf course couldn't imagine. The race director, confused, asked casually if they golfed. Phoebe and Harold, wiping their eyes, both said no, emphatically, at the very same time and that coincidence made them laugh again and they delved back into that silly turbulence.

After a day of incredible filth and angles, really, though, it was the delirium of contrast. They couldn't even imagine this sport. On their way driving back in through town, thirsty and famished, Harold had insisted that they stop at a wand wash to clean off their bikes before anything else. Dirt unnerved him, but particularly on his bicycle, which was white because he was the sort of guy who could care for a white bicycle. Once their bikes were clean and they were back at the dorm rooms, Phoebe had found various sorts of dust and loam were embedded in the chamois of her cycling shorts. Grime was thick between her toes, crammed in places where dirt didn't belong. Now, the even grass before them appeared supersaturated. That carpet of perfect golf green stretched out to the horizon pleasingly, framed by trees and mountains, sometimes interrupted by oval-shapes that were slightly paler golf green. Phoebe, stupefied by hunger and fatigue, thought about how the language to describe manufactured nature circled back on itself, the greens being both a place that had a colour and a colour that had a place. The greens were immaculately green. Golf green golf greens.

It was a marvel so perfectly constructed she did not want to look away. And when animated by these comedic humans, foolish in their follies, it was an absurd paradise.

The food, when it arrived, was obviously mediocre but tasted incredible. The wine was spectacularly overpriced but delicious. Phoebe was even pleased by the ice water. Those little slices of lemon! It all disappeared quickly. As soon as the server cleared the plates, the race director insisted on paying the bill. Too bad. Phoebe felt she could have eaten forever. Another round of everything!

The other group of cyclists had been put at a table indoors and had not asked to move outside. When they were done eating, though, the other half of their entourage came over to occupy the outdoor couches beside Phoebe and Harold's table, thinking they would all hang out. The race director and the photographer decided to turn in – they had an early morning, they averred, as if it weren't the same morning for everyone – so that left just Phoebe and Harold. The two turned their chairs around so they could visit with the others, so clean in their street clothing.

Soon Phoebe stood up and started talking about the golf-green-side alcohol service, the theatrics the others had missed, and how incredible this sport was to her, imitating just a little the men that she had seen trying to play golf at that point in the day. She was good at physical comedy. The crowd was properly entertained by the impression, and so Phoebe also laughed. She added a coda to her routine, and the laughter was louder. Guy, seated furthest away, stared at her with puppy-like adoration. His soul patch gleamed in the gas fireplace's heroic glow. Then the server returned to scold them for combining dining groups, which Phoebe assumed meant her standing beside one of the woven-plastic armchairs while she did her routine. Only six people per table, the server insisted.

Even if we put our chairs at a different table and we're just talking at afar at each other? asked Phoebe.

Yes, said the server, fiddling with his mask. I'm sorry, but that's the rule.

Phoebe and Harold opted not for another round of drinks. If they weren't allowed to talk with the others, what was the point? The sun was nearly gone, and a mountain chill descended. They could be alone together in the hotel room. There, the thin pillows folded behind their necks, Harold used his iPad to watch the pandemic-edition of the Tour de France, truncated and at the wrong time of year. Phoebe half-watched and found while Googling on her phone that the original Tegarts, a set of Irish brothers, had married into the Indigenous population; now Tegart was a common Indigenous last name. The pass could have just as easily be named for them, at least in our minds, she mused. Does that make sense?

Uh huh, concurred Harold, eyes glued to the screen. Some new cycling talent was madly descending the most serpentine route, crouched with his belly on the top tube, carving gloriously aggressive lines. A graphic at the bottom of the screen showed how many seconds he was putting into the gap back to the peloton. The number was ascending rapidly, seconds flipping into minutes. It was an astonishing performance.

I guess it depends on whether a landmark asks you to think about the present or the past. It's an insult to think that a colonial name is anything but an emblem of colonialism.

But maybe today-Tegarts are proud that their hybridity is celebrated?

And what about white South Africans? she continued. She was thinking of Guy, his confusing allure, his predictable but myopically awful position on South African land reform. The land, after all, was being redistributed to the Blacks after it had been *taken from them*. It was bad for international commerce, evidently, but no one actually thought that capitalism was a reliable moral compass, did they? Or do white South Africans generally fail to account for their racial privilege? How do you cope with your legacy of privilege?

Harold shrugged. He muttered, how does anyone, though? Then his toes nudging towards hers under the blanket as he did when he wanted to turn off the lights and stop talking and go to sleep.

Day 3

Sunday was a new day. Phoebe woke up in white sheets on a firm mattress and was pleased by this thought of the morning. She drew the curtains and admired how the sun was coming up over the jagged horizon. The panorama of Panorama. The reality, however, was a terror. For one, outside was paralyzingly chilly. Plus, overnight, smoke from wildfires in the northwestern United States had drifted over the border. The orange light was filtered and cold and thick. It had a flavour that, as they drove to meet the group, pervaded into the car, despite the doors and windows being sealed shut.

At breakfast, at the same Tim Hortons, Harold now capitulated and ordered something greasy to eat. With a large cup of coffee, double skim milk. He ate the food, a sandwich, and a hash brown, unhappily. His lips did not quite reach around the food as he bit down.

In the half circle they formed in the parking lot, the cyclists listened to the race director explain the day's plan. They would take a turn off from the highway – where there was no excuse to turn off the highway, that is what it would look like – onto a mining road. He had been warned that mining trucks might come down the road, that it was "radio-only" access but since they didn't have radios, just permission, they'd need to be extra careful. This was because the road was only wide enough for one vehicle at a time. If they encountered oncoming traffic, they'd have to reverse to one of the pull-outs.

The forest fire smoke had really come in overnight. The fires weren't even close, being an international border and two states over, but now that they were standing outside, the taste of ash settled decisively into their tongues.

Climate change, muttered Harold. People think it's about unseasonably warm temperatures but, really, it's about the increased frequency of natural disasters.

As they ate their unhealthful breakfasts, one of the other women, the woman who had been so friendly and had gestured for Phoebe to sit beside her on the outdoor couch last night, drove up to the parking lot a bit erratically. She swerved into a stall then rushed out of the car and sprinted into the bushes. Phoebe started laughing because it was so weird. Then she saw that the woman was vomiting, hunched over and badly aiming for the shrubbery. This is the part in a plague movie, thought Phoebe at once, not without disrelish, when it really begins.

The professor had gone home late last night, too, the race organizer explained. His son's class was going into quarantine. Professor wanted to be there to support him. This, Phoebe observed, was also cinematic. The heroic male figure running directly towards contagion. This one always inexplicably survives, recovering on the potent fuel of parental loyalty.

The vomiting woman returned from the bushes, all apologies. Phoebe and Harold took matching steps backwards as she rejoined the circle. I'm fine, she declared. Just a bad energy bar yesterday.

With that, they set off. On the highway just outside of town, however, the sick woman pulled over her car and knelt in the ditch. There, she heaved gooey strings. Another of the cyclists stopped and rushed out to see her. Phoebe had Harold park on the shoulder and he put on his hazard lights. She tried to text the race organizer to let him know that they were delayed, but they were in a dead zone for cell reception.

This is how everyone dies of hydrogen sulfide poisoning, isn't it? said Phoebe. One person goes down, another goes to check. Everyone is so compassionate. This is awful. I don't want her to die, but I also don't run towards disaster. Am I awful?

Yes, said Harold.

What?

Yes, that's how people die of hydrogen sulfide poisoning. It's the first thing that they teach you when you are going to go into the field. Ignore your instincts to run towards the danger. Seriously, it's how a lot of people end up dying when there's an H2S leak. One person goes down, another goes to check, goes down, and another. The bodies pile up.

Energy bars don't go bad, either, said Phoebe. Ever. At worst, they dry out.

The caravan was waiting at their turnoff, where the radio-only road began. Finally, the ill woman conceded that she'd be better off heading home. Phoebe felt relief. The race organizer plied her with a sponsor's energy drink. Get those electrolytes back in balance, he advised firmly.

They continued onto the mining road, a wide, white ribbon of fine white dust through infinite depths of thick forests. Settlers' Road, it was called. The conifers on either side of the gravel road were chalked with the same chalky silt that covered the road. The effect was ghostly. Sometimes Phoebe watched horror films, never in English, and Harold, who only spoke English, would agree to watch, but, really, he would spend most of his time on his phone. It was a tacit accord. They had just watched one in French, a television series, whose serial killer was some sort of demented half human, half deer. This type of show is what Harold called "Phoebe catnip." It was weird, it was subtitled, the lead was a woman, and the plot was equal parts hammy and rococo. That French forest was similarly ominous, similarly impenetrable. *Forest* green. (The forests in Alberta were aspen parkland, a brighter and yellower shade of green that wasn't forest green. Somehow, this was less intimidating.) Because Harold had been on Instagram for the two seasons of the television show, he wasn't making the connection.

No one would ever find a body that was left out there, Phoebe commented idly. Like, anything could happen in there. No one would ever have any idea.

I suppose that is true, replied Harold, focussed more on driving safely than comparing the woods to horror films. The cars in front were sending up massive plumes of fine silt into the air. Though Harold was following just far enough back that the clouds of dust from the car ahead didn't completely obscure his vision, Phoebe's nose had become clotted with clay, and silt was accumulating on the dashboard.

The photoshoot was located, implausibly, at the end of this "settlers' road." They arrived, finally, without encountering other traffic, and parked in a gravel lot in front of a homey Nordic ski lodge. Ancient indoor furniture mildewed under an awning. Over there, a disc golf course. From the silt-coated cars, the others emerged. Their bikes were all chalk. The air was spectacularly cold.

Yikes, said Phoebe as she got out of the car. It's not quite warm out, eh? She put her down jacket on top of all of her other clothing and slipped on another pair of pants.

Guy thought her comment was hilarious. Phoebe did not, but she appreciated the attention. Guy wore cycling shorts, because he was a guy like that.

Who are you? Phoebe asked him loudly and jestfully. Underdressing in comparison with the Canadians even, are you?

None of that, he said, simply smiling. I forgot my leg warmers at home. I didn't expect it to be like this. What is summer in this place?

Not very summery, quipped Harold quickly. This was one of the things he knew to be true. He hated the cold. Couldn't we live somewhere that doesn't try to kill us, he would plead sometimes. Where the air doesn't hurt to breathe. Usually he said this mid-winter when the air was legitimately cold, minus twenty-five or thirty, but sometimes it was a rhetorical complaint. Today, however, he only dug out his down vest.

The others were also finding gloves and toques and insulated pants. Then the photoshoot happened, which, once more, was dull. The owner of the lodges came out to watch while the photographer picked groups of riders to traverse a field. First the women, then combinations of men and women that seemed aesthetic, then just the men. Phoebe could not follow the logic, but she did what she was told to do. The race organizer went with the lodge owner to chat. One of the nights, the stage race would stop here. Cyclists would either sleep in the log cabins or camp in the meadow. The lodge owner was a stout man in his sixties or seventies and all old timer-y, with a plaid shirt and suspenders and worn denim. He had a grey beard and a silly hat. The look reminded Phoebe of a cartoon prospector.

The thing, he was saying, holding his smug thumbs in those silly suspenders, is that the coronavirus has only a point-three percent mortality rate. It's just another flu! The average age of death from coronavirus is eighty-three, which is the average life expectancy in our province. Figure me that. Sure, the liberal media would have you believe different, but the truth is something else.

Nope, thought Phoebe firmly, and she left to watch the other cyclists traverse the field. The photographer was having them pretend to do a race effort. This, in itself, was odd because this field was where the camping was going to be. Maybe he didn't realize that. The situation was worsened by the repetitions. The guys kept telling some jokes that were crippling their race faces. Stop having so much fun! the photog shouted. You're meant to be racing! Meanwhile, the drone buzzed and whirred overhead. Suddenly, though, the machine went rogue, drifting away towards the high branches of a tree. At once, people scurried to locate it.

This place was another destination, another about which Phoebe had been curious. Like Panorama, this was one of the places that people with money went to, those with the humble sort of money. They came for cross-country skiing in the winter. Cross-country skiers, she had noticed, categorically acted threadbare until it was time to go on vacation. From this resort, they returned with hushed and reverential accounts. The trails were spectacular. The views unmissable. The cabins, the height of rough-hewn luxury. No one mentioned the owner, or the perilous drive in (although, Phoebe speculated, the mines probably didn't operate in the winter).

The views now, however, were clogged with the wildfire smoke. Phoebe wandered over to the cabins, whose porches were coated with the same silt that coated everything else. She tried out a rattan rocking chair, tapping her cycling cleats against the wooden floor as she rocked back and forth. Soon Harold and Guy joined her. The two men were thick in a conversation about Guy's inventiveness. They had found they really liked each other.

Phoebe loved when this happened. While Harold had raced bikes in Japan, in the years that they had known each other but were not a couple, she had done all sorts of other things. By the time she arrived in a monogamous relationship, Phoebe felt only relief. But while she had indulged, Harold had not done all sorts of things throughout his twenties: he had only ridden bicycles. So, sometimes women would fawn on him, and Phoebe would roll her eyes. Sure. Watching him flirt, try to flirt, reminded her of how much she appreciated his clumsy charms. That was nice enough. Sometimes men would meet him, though, and this was completely different. Their desire for him seemed so pure. They wanted only *want.* They wanted him. The men were the same: tall and thin like him. Handsome. When they saw him, their mouths opened just a little and their eyes softened and gleamed. The lust was palpable. She could appreciate this. Harold was not interested in men, but this was also the beauty of desire. Guy looked at Harold like this, too, starrily.

One of the reasons that Guy had come to Canada, she learned in listening to their conversation, was to develop an alternative to carbon fibre. Carbon fibre was the stuff of the lightest but also stiffest bicycle frames and components. Everyone knew that. But he had figured out that you could make a similar fibre out of a plant. This would be more ecological. The two spoke of elastomers and tensile strength. Complicated chemical processes. Transformations. The nonsense vocabulary, nonsense to Phoebe at least, was fantastic and intricate. All she could see, really, was how totally engrossed they were with each other.

Off, over there, the mineral blue stream gurgled. The powdery silt looked like snow on its banks. Someone's bicycle computer read that it was five degrees Celsius. The light through the clog of smoke was orange-tinted and warming. There were a lot of things going on with this day.

You'd think we could go for a quick dip? she asked, pointing over there, not at all serious. I'm coated in this dust.

Oh, said Guy, perking up, did we bring our swimsuits?

I'm wearing mine right now, in fact, replied Harold. Under my kit.

It's a G-string now, is it? Guy asked, smoothly. He tilted his head to glance at Harold's butt.

Indeed, said Harold a little more softly, it is.

They didn't swim. Of course not. The glacial-fed streams looked tempting, but the cold was otherworldly. The three of them stayed put on the porch and discussed ecological alternatives to carbon fibre and the adventures of industry and capital as if they were united and true believers.

Eventually, the photographer ambled over, through the lumpy grassy meadow, past the rusting playground equipment for absent children, and knelt to snap photos of them together. These are great, he insisted. Even though the lighting under the porch was dim and their faces were pinched with the cold, and they were wearing altogether too much clothing for the imaginary July that they were meant to be inhabiting. Phoebe knew in advance they wouldn't be great photos. But she nodded and smiled at the lens, manoeuvring her heart to span that inevitable gulf between an object and its representation, and then back again.

Years later, when they are in the midst of a passionately angry argument about something unrelated, their lives now oriented differently, strung with tethers of other virtues, on a landscape whose foliage dances defiantly against the prevailing winds, Harold will ask if Phoebe has ever been unfaithful to him. His voice billows with rage.

Just once, Phoebe will say, her entire being enraged back at Harold. She will hiss at him: With Guy.

But what guy? Harold will ask.

Guy. You know. *Guy*.

The words clot in her throat. Then they will nosedive back into whatever argument they were having before and the topic will fall, engulfed in other furies. Phoebe will briefly have the image of those photos flash through her mind, when they came back weeks afterward, how her face was scowling in all of them, how the lighting was just as bad as she feared. None of the magic that she felt or recalled was on display, just the dull sadness that tinted all those days. The secret of their fumbling pursuit towards something better, something more magnanimous or magnificent, uncaptured. Why was the valiant trajectory so opaque and ugly?

When things calm again, as they always do, Harold will hold that jagged shard of a revelation tightly. He'll not know how to bring it up again without uncapping turmoil that he does not want to let run amok again with Phoebe. She remains, after all, his beloved. His dearest. He will think about their years together, all the guys that they have known in the many years who have been close, how every night their bodies curved beside each other and how his world lived in that proximity of skin, and wonder when and how this could have happened. With which guy.

Miette is for Optimists

The drive to the hot springs is always longer through the trees than I expect – some seventeen kilometres up, according to the green Parks Canada road signs, a twisting mountain road. Except for the viewpoint partway along, overlooking a valley, the route consists solely of conifers and swerve. Stan is driving. He grew up in interior BC, so he is taking the turns a little faster than I would. One hand on the steering wheel, two o'clock. I try to sip from my water bottle and splash water in my face instead. Stan doesn't notice. His eyes are fixated on the road. Music plays off his phone into the car stereo, a confection playlist, Vampire Weekend and Taylor Swift. He sings the choruses softly and his fingers, on the wheel, tap along.

Eventually, the forest breaks a little, and the road becomes gravelly, and it's hard not to think that this is the end of the road. But then the sightlines open up more, and it keeps going. Soon, touristic log cabins appear on the left and then a massive parking lot arcs off to the right.

Like any destination in the national park, once you're there, you're there, and tour buses are, too.

We take our things and go to wait in line while a light drizzle falls. The clouds are low hung. Whole families shuffle about taking photos while clutching towels. Stan fingers his phone for a while but neither of us has reception. Well, he says.

I look at him. He's in this Carhartt jacket that might suggest that he is a rancher, maybe, or someone who works with his hands. He is not. No one who wears a Carhartt jacket professionally would mistake him, either, I don't think. He's too spritely, too lithe, too eager to the task. The actual tradespeople we know get the job done but are chill about it. Stan puts on this jacket, and then he's *ready*. There's nothing he loves more than building fences. He lives for it. Measuring twice, cutting once, excavating holes. The whole nine metres of it. No, the jacket was a gift from a friend whose belly outgrew it. Stan is sentimental about his friends, so he loves this jacket. The cuffs are fraying, and the canvas is speckled with paint. It's not the best fit on him, unsurprisingly, either – his frame is so tiny – but that doesn't matter. He keeps it in his car throughout the summer as the clutch layer for fire pits and backyard beers. Having vastly forgotten how cold the mountains are relative to the city, however, he has been wearing it since a blustery gas station stop in Hinton. Now, Stan shoves his phone into one of the big, utility pockets and taps a sneaker impatiently against a concrete pillar. Why, he says, are there so many people here? The weather is junk.

But we're also here, I point out.

He shrugs and continues to rap his foot against the pillar.

No, Stan is obviously a desk worker because, for instance, our car. It is a Volvo, not an F-150. Sometimes we scream our proclivities out loud. Like with this Volvo. It is seven years old. Similarly, take his aspirations for our next car. On the drive here, he was going on about replacing it with a hybrid. (A Volvo Volt? I asked, knowing nothing about electric cars. It would be, I continue to riff, an e-volvo-tion of the car industry?

An electric Volvo should be called a Volt, he agreed happily. But, he added, Chevy got to that one first.)

Anyway, he isn't going to be buying a new car. Not an electric, not a hybrid, not even a more fuel-efficient gas guzzler. Nope to all of it. We are the sort of couple that is going to go from having a current small-l liberal car to an ageing small-l liberal car. It might push us into a different political identity altogether. A ten-year-old Volvo, when you think about it, is so pro-union.

You may have guessed at this point that I don't care much about cars, and this is true.

At last, we arrive at the head of the line. I rent a unisex "heritage" suit. A swimsuit sounds like a questionable garment to share with strangers, but these are made of bombproof polyester that withstand (what I imagine is) the most thorough sterilization. No, I am just not bothered by it. They're navy blue and white and tough. Two dollars. I am a 1920s movie star. I am connecting with a heritage of our nation.

Not having forgotten his swim trunks, Stan does not take this up. All he would think about is the residual germs. I know this about him.

Poolside, the vista is worthy of postcards. There are the four pools, scenically arranged: a hot tub, a hotter tub, and two cold pools. Babies splash through the first one, which is shallow and always bathwater warm. Beet-shaded adults idle in the next, neck-deep in water and steam pluming around their faces. It was hard to summon the bravery to think of the plunge pools. One cool, the other icy. Around us, the mountains.

An uncanny feeling hits me. For a moment, I feel as if I have been here before. I mean, I have. But you know what I mean. This ill-tempered day, the throng of people lost in mist and water. The gloomy mountains. The way that the angles feel all wrong – the heights too high and the forests too close to the pool. The way the mountains lurk with sullen indifference. Nature is beautiful and all, but Stan likes to remind anyone who will listen that the Romantic poets, when they spoke about sublimity, were talking about the sort of beauty that also terrifies. (He was one of three guys in this university course, the only Asian man, which he confesses he took because he thought poetry should be romantic. But, though none of the university girlfriends he met in that class worked out, he has made hay of the course material.) Today, with the loose, wet clouds smeared all over the mountain scape, the crush of dark evergreen trees invading our sightlines, I think: yes. I agree.

A new patter of rain stings my just-showered skin, and Stan, having emerged from the change room, nudges me. Then we, too, head to the water. Casually, he drops into the deep end of the hottest pool. I climb down the ladder instead, deliciously submerging, and stand on my toes. Stan's hair gets dunked and spiky and glistens black. He wraps his hands around me under water. It is perfect.

In June, shortly after his forty-fifth birthday, Stan declared that he was done. That his formation was complete. He would quit reading. Or almost quit. His process into monasticism was deeply hypocritical from the get-go, is what I'm saying. He would still crack his laptop to the *New York Times* website in the morning. The six o'clock news on the radio, when he pinballed around the kitchen, cooking altogether too elaborate meals for a weeknight, was no-talking time so he could catch up on the day's news. Even though he was already caught up because his phone sent him breaking news alerts from the CBC and the *Guardian* and the *New York Times*, too. In different alert tones, even, which he refused to put on silent. But books, who needs them, he declared. It wasn't a commitment to newfound ignorance, he was careful to argue (his capacity for debate was totally untouched by these developments), but a completist declaration. His philosophical formation had occurred years ago. Continuing to pretend otherwise was farcical.

Coincidentally, he had just lost his job as a geochemist. (It was not a coincidence.) These were not easy days. Over these dinners, meticulously finished with fresh herbs and a dance of squeezed lemon, he'd go over it again. His work had been at a private company that, he said, had no scruples. He had been no idiot. Workplaces were not family – that was just capitalistic rhetoric in action. (Please pass the pepper. Do you think the capers were a good idea?) The whole *point* is to paper over social relations, the actual power dynamics between employer and employee, to obtain labour's surplus. Of course, you'll work harder if you think you're part of a family!

He didn't talk like this before they had let him go. When he worked there, he loved his coworkers. Loved! It's a big word! But he did love them. They were weird people, to me, but I had never spent much time around geochemists. I did not love them, but I accepted they were his kind of weird.

And, they – cerebral, socially inept, patient – were undeniably likeable humans. So I liked them. It's easier to like people, anyway. It's an economics of emotional energy.

One night in August, when Stan was still smarting from his newfound unemployment, we went to the house of his cubicle mate for a get-together. Former cubicle mate. The evening was muggy and buggy. We went to the backyard to drink gin and tonics from mason jars. I had worn a yellow sundress and soon regretted it. Perched on the ancient wooden patio furniture that had come with the house, we were awkward, but me particularly so because of the stupid dress. I was being eaten alive. *Eaten!*

Around us, their dog, a rescue mutt, bounded frenetically. The bench that I had creaked and shifted each time I crossed my legs, my bare skin eroding pain flecks into the night. The dog barked at anything. He kept romping up to me and burying his snout in my crotch. The others were apologetic and barked at him to be more polite. Have some manners! they chided, entreaties which were comically ineffectual. Dogs don't speak English! Meanwhile, I slapped more mosquitoes off my welted skin.

Stan's cubicle mate was a meek redhead, Andrew, who began to ready a fire. Former cubicle mate. His hobbies included playing clarinet and growing cacti. By habit, his hands clung to his sides like a tyrannosaurus. All the better to noodle on the licorice stick, he guffawed, when Stan lightly razed him about it. That week, Andrew had purchased a silver-coloured canister, which he set in the centre of our circle – the future of backyard fires, he averred. Look at how the metal directs all the smoke upwards, while the outside stays cool.

Andrew's spouse, Marsha, was also weird. She had long, dirty blonde hair that framed a moon-shaped face and wore glasses that made her green eyes look goggly and fish-like. Her main character trait, according to me, was her total and blind faith in the conceit of the middle class. Relationships had to progress according to strict rules, a progression onto which couples had to hang their progressive materialistic accomplishments. She was practically rabid about this. That invariable syntax of dating, marriage, cohabitation, dog ownership, home buying. Children. Of course, as with any all-absorbing conceit, there were cracks. Her previous partner, for instance, a professional unicyclist (there is such a thing? Stan interrupted; she only glared at him in response), occupied no small amount of air in the household. He had not been ready for this stage in his life. He didn't know what he wanted. He did not know how to put the relationship first. Andrew nodded along, crashing small branches over his knee for kindling. He did know what he wanted. They both did.

It was this: a tastefully renovated, mid-century bungalow. A deliberately nice neighbourhood, with tree-lined boulevards and shiny-safe playgrounds, with walkable coffee shops and modern restaurants. Season tickets to the symphony and an auto-renewing membership at the Art Gallery of Alberta. Monogamy and couples dates. A backyard with an apple tree and a cedar fence strung with white Christmas lights year-round. Friends over on a Friday for drinks, where everyone might bask, beneath those all-season lights, in the serenity and security of the upper middle class. The soft, white light suffused the entire evening. Soon, Andrew got the fire blazing, and we were edging towards tipsy. The gin was from a local distillery, and the drinks were stiff. Stan, who hadn't exactly been the life of the party much in those days, started cracking jokes. How nice, I thought, between unfamiliar, juicy crescendos of laughter. The fire cast an agreeable amber light over our elation. I noticed that when Andrew laughed, his lower lip moved but his upper lip just trembled. In contrast, Marsha didn't laugh at all. She stared at us through those thick glasses, watching us carefully. It felt as if our behaviour had ventured well past her sense of the familiar.

Then, to our surprise, she darted over to the garage and pulled out her unicycle. It was a high-end model that she had purchased as a "hers" to the "his-and-hers" of when she was with that one-time professional off-road unicyclist. She had, she explained now, upbeat, loved unicycling as a child! When they were together, it made sense for her to have one that could keep up with him. She explained this as she rolled the single, thick knobby tire toward the fire. The machine had its own disc brake, even. Look. For descents. Then she pulled out a trio of large knives from a nylon sheath. Holding the knives in one hand, she mounted on the unicycle and started riding in a small, jagged circle in the yard. Then she started to juggle the knives.

They weren't real, she was careful to assure us, as the blades flipped in her hands, because no one ever really juggled real knives. They were dull, just illusions of knife-ness. The blades flashed reflections of the fire pit. Sweat beaded on her orange-lit face. Andrew asked if she wanted him to start putting the old wood patio furniture into the blaze. But we're sitting on it, I protested. Marsha cheerfully advised us to do what we thought best. She continued rotating about, juggling with intention. They had been together for eighteen months and were trying for a child. This is what she told me in the kitchen when we were pouring our gin and tonics, and she was making a mocktail. IVF. It wasn't happening fast enough. She could see forty on the horizon.

In the months after Stan lost his job – a major client had transferred their business to a competitor, and there was a small and brutal evacuation of employees – friends like Andrew and Marsha soon stopped being our friends. This was our fault, no question. Stan was really something else, especially at the beginning. So cranky, so argumentative. He managed to alienate Andrew, whom I had assumed was fundamentally unalienable, but he did. It was even a texting argument. To me, that had seemed additionally absurd. There's a difference, commented Stan, between brute nihilism and the emptiness that leaves space for grace to enter.

Yes, I agreed, without thinking about it. I mean, why not?

Truthfully, I preferred our social monasticism. Our predictable world was exhausting. Couples worked good jobs, had children at appropriate moments, put them into daycare, lauded their small humans' irreducible brilliance once they hit school, and scheduled them into cello and soccer (or whatever musical instrument and sport combination was idiosyncratically resonant). They complained about how busy they were but nonetheless continued enviable career trajectories. They bought a vacation property and did so even while saving for retirement at an even pace. The women's foreheads froze into a Botoxed sheen at thirty-five. The men went bald, or bald-ish, grew paunchy and distinguished, and their wives nonetheless loved them faithfully. The women turned forty and celebrated with girls' weekends at resorts in Tofino, where they rented mountain bicycles to pedal along tame boardwalks by the ocean, or watched whales from the vantage of small but expensive watercraft. I didn't know how we had arrived here, exactly, but I didn't belong.

Whatever.

The hot tub was tepid, honestly. The rain lightened but it didn't stop. This fact didn't damper the enthusiasm of anyone in the floating crowd. The wet pinging did become easier to ignore in time. A woman ebbed past in a string bikini. The thing about being here, in a national park, is that people are almost always from somewhere else. I enjoyed watching and guessing. The foreigners with the unfamiliar labels on outdoor gear. The city folks blurting primary colours in nylon: yellow pants, blue jacket, red pants.

A woman, with her evenly tanned skin and with her hair in one of those dashed-together-but-perfect buns – I pegged her as maybe a nurse, probably small-town. The man I assumed was her husband, a drab Latino, definitely hot when he was younger, was just another person in the trades. Probably oil and gas, because what else was there? Two children, little grinning carbon copies of the man, tangled with each other in the water nearby.

Then I heard some languid France-French slang. Another flock of kids were slinging in Franglais to propose a "quick dip" in the cool pool. For a while, I listened to them chat, the whole crowd of them with dark-tossed hair, boys. The two smaller ones spoke with a slight English accent. The older two, maybe in their late teens, were really French. I guessed they were cousins. The younger ones were on about playing basketball at school, then hockey, then video games. The older boys' interest, distant yet genuine, charitable, caught my attention. Their kindness surprised me. Is this how boys are? I had no idea.

Coucou, les enfants! said a dark-haired woman who appeared cheerfully and lowered into the waters, into the thick throng of boys. Soon, another woman came, her hair badly dyed, with a cinderblock jaw and Easter-Island nose. For a moment, I drew lines between their features and the children. To me, it felt less interesting that the children weren't their own society, sprung from the waters fully formed and independent.

Stan wasn't that into hot tubs, but he had developed a thing for cold water exposure. There is a guy on the internet convinced that cold water exposure is the key to all sorts of wonder and self-bolstering. Concentration, immune system, youth. He touts phrases like, "I'm not afraid of death, I'm afraid of not having lived life fully." He boasts about defying science. About how to break through your perceived limits and discover new mental and physical ground. When I looked at his website and read the *Outside* magazine article about him, it felt more like a demographic moment than a revelation. Middle-aged man rediscovers vitality? A tale as old as time!

To me, the guy, to be uncharitable about it, was a cliché. Him, with his shaggy grey beard, a ponytail clearly compensating for his head of perilously thinning hair, posed with ice water dripping from his thick-pored face. Stan chided me for my scepticism. My pessimism. He was left to raise four kids after his wife committed suicide, for heaven's sake, said Stan. (I wanted to reply: but did he *really* raise the kids, or did a woman or a bunch of women intervene to save him from the task?

No, I decided, I will not, and I bit my tongue.) Battling with myself, I finally said instead: What an admirable spirit of reinvention!

Anyway, Stan also didn't like lakes, even cold lakes, because of the microorganisms that lurked in the water. Logic could not defeat this position, as logic rarely does combat when you want it to. Today, he could practise cold water immersion while I got to stay warm in the mineral hot springs. He pecked me on the lips and went to do that, a complicated process of breathing and dunking that I didn't need to witness. Instead, I floated into the deeper area and paddled in slow circles on my back.

There was the woman, again, though, the one in the scant swimsuit, the one with her family. She was perched on the edge of the pool while her children bobbed and dunked in the deep end. Wisps of perfect hair, untangled from her bun, were damp on the ends. Otherwise, she was immaculate, her makeup unsmudged. Her breasts were strange, though. Two far-spaced scoops on her chest. Strange, I thought, obliviously, and my eyes lingered. Eventually, like an idiot, I realized what it really was: a terrible boob job. I regarded the mediocre husband, his paunch and his fading tattoos, who was tossing the smaller one of the children up and down now, not far away, and I wasn't sure whether to be depressed about this.

Then a teenager was beating on another teenager, really flailing him in the cool pool. Their commotion attracted attention, with enough splashing that a lifeguard was already speed-walking over to intervene. A shaggy, fair-haired kid and the other with shorter, dark hair. Both tall and lithe and muscled. Amidst their flurry of elbows, I did a double take. The shaggy one had gone to school with my son. An electric ache stunned my chest. The other was his older brother. I started scanning for their parents, who must also be there. How unrecognizable the kids were. I had forgotten how that happened, children metamorphosing, day over day. But these kids as teenagers. Wow.

The parents were more unchanged. I saw them at the other end of the hot pool and began to swim through a mess of people to say hello. I didn't know what I was going to say to them. But I had always liked the mother. Unlike most of the other women at my son's school, she had worked through children, pursuing a minor career compared to her husband, sure, who was a big shot at the university studying climate change. But she had insisted that her work receive something resembling equal resources at home, which made her stand out in the kindergarten pickup crowd of doctor's wives and nannies. Now I moved through the rain and the steam. These nearly naked bodies. Up close, I saw the husband was now withering, grey and soft and stooped. His chest and arms were curlicues of white hair. I hugged the wife. Her blond highlights were finesse.

Time had also excavated me, but we didn't talk about that. I also felt granularly transformed. I could point to the proof. These wrinkles. These grey hairs. This dismay of flesh.

But my proof, unlike theirs, really gestured at nothing.

Anyway, they were in the mountains to backpack the Skyline, a cheerful and determined family doing it together. The boys didn't like it that much at the time, confessed the wife, particularly with the weather up on the notch, which was snow-sleeting. But they had persevered. This was the reward. A good soak. What hale children they were.

But, she asked, did you hear? Someone shot a bear on the Skyline.

This was apparently the talk of the town, but I had missed it. The two of them filled me in. Stan and I hadn't had reliable cell phone coverage for days. We hadn't been reading the news. Someone, explained the husband and wife in flurried tandem, had come across a bear on the trail and decided to shoot it. On the spot. The bear didn't die, but was knocked off an embankment, down into thick forest. Blood all over the place. No one saw the bear again. Maybe it was angry, maybe it was dead.

You're not even allowed guns in national parks, the husband remarked. What were they thinking?

Who had guns? I mean, for the longest time, I thought no one owned guns, that it was just a mythological aspect of the province, but then I realized it was another type of litmus, one that no one really talked about, announcing one's political proclivities. I just lived in a leftist bubble. Then I assumed that no one really used them. Eventually, however, I started paying attention and saw that I was wrong again. They did. This was another demarcation of aging in a specific political alignment: becoming ethically responsible for one's meat consumption. Once, we canoed a lake, inadvertently, on the first day of duck hunting season. I had joked about how fake a wooden decoy looked. Not long after, the water skittled with bullets. It was a fraught, high-cadence paddle back to the shore, shouting our humanity out to the open air, hoping our voices would carry.

But I nonetheless thought that there was a certain unspoken etiquette to guns. You don't take them backpacking in national parks. You don't shoot bears, I said aloud. The two nodded in emphatic agreement.

In the past, I had bashed heads, almost categorically, with the husband. He was so used to being right. One of those men who assumed he was the smartest person in the room. It just irked me. I suppose someone might say we shared these attributes. Stan called it "catnip" the way that I took it upon myself to take men like him down a notch. I tried to resist. Really. Once, the three of us – the wife, the husband, and I – we got drunk over dinner at their house. Conversation became a debate, old-school style with no Googling, about which prime ministers appointed which judges to the Supreme Court. I should say, it was me versus the husband. (The wife, the partner at an interior design firm, wisely stayed out of the fray.) Our teeth were purple fangs. Harper or Chretien! Mulroney or Joe Clark! Trudeau *père* or Trudeau *fils*! Eventually, in a moment of delirious detente, we consulted the internet. On every point of contention, I was right.

The victory, frankly, felt delicious.

Now, he was going on, in moralistic tones, about guns and wildlife and it was unthinkable that we wouldn't all agree on it. I stopped listening and my eyes lost focus at that thick forest. My son had become sick, and that was when

I disappeared. This lively tapestry, of debate and wine and children ignored past bedtime in front of animated movies, wasn't mine anymore. I submerged into that dark pond of caregiving. I drowned in that watered-down oblivion. Resuscitate what women you want from the pantheon of literature or art – the reality is that they don't exist, and if they do exist, they don't have children. Ours are small canvases. I used to think it was a cliché. But then my world narrowed. And at the centre, was my son. Until he wasn't.

Then Stan returned from the cold pool. Rivulets of cold water pulsed down his chest and across the orange nylon waistband of his swim shorts.

The hot water is daggers! he yelped. He grabbed me with his hands of cold rubber and lowered himself deeper. To the husband, he conferred in the way that men talk with each other, and I always feel relief because I don't have to care. Stan didn't even know him; these were people from my before times. Later, eventually, the conversation ebbed, and they had to go anyway. Later, Stan convinced me to try the cold pool and the funny panting-at-ice-cubes breathing and, while I didn't like it, I also didn't complain.

That evening, we went back to the pine cabin, the pine cabin that was meant to be romantic in some sense that we both imagined, but then we were there in a small room, and it was just us, as it was always just us, and we seemed to feel neither more or less about each other than we ever did. Mercifully, by habit, we felt quite a bit. That was our even keel: a deep, fundamental like. And so that evening in the pine cabin, mounted on Stan, my mind drifted for a moment, and

I thought about what they felt like, those ice-cream-scoop boobs. I thought about bold disfiguration, how it blurred into eros. The glazed wood panelling held the moonlight in its gloss. The Athabasca River gurgled white noise secrets aloud. Texture was magnificent. I surged with it.

When I slept, it continued. I dreamt about a chest in front of me – a woman displaying herself for my benefit, two immaculate sunny-side-up eggs on her chest. I reached my hand out, knowing that they would be as my breasts are, as egg yolks are, bright and deceptively insubstantial. They looked like breasts, or something like breasts, but they were not. Look at me. Mine are really just breast-shaped skin, with wilted nipples. The consistency of nothing. In my dream, as my hand hesitated above her amplified chest, I thought about how I would break those yolks if I were to touch them. A dangerous gloss to puncture. A gush of orange temptation. My brave hand hovered.

I woke up. Our wood panelled walls were momentarily foreign. Stan still slept beneath white sheets. Outside, I saw morning suggesting itself against a skyline of tall rocks. What a confection, I thought upon waking in this perfect cabin in the perfect mountains.

Modern Times

Benji started off his midlife crisis in a favourable way. The early November morning was dingy, clouded with the idea of snow or rain. It was his birthday. He was in New York. Half-tangled in duvet, his New York girlfriend furiously fellated him.

There were, he thought in gasps, *worse* ways to grow old.

Jen was too good for him. This was implicit, this was their pact, their mutual understanding. Her: a successful New Yorker, who ran her own business and made time for exercise and charity. Also, gorgeous. Smart. Funny. Him: a single dad and a compliance officer in a mid-sized oil and gas firm, Northern Canada. She *arranged flowers* by day and made a living of it. Like, seriously. He pushed paper and drove kids to hockey practice. Their relationship was implausible. But, yet, it was not. Here it was. The proof of it was right now.

And now, as his hand moved on her warm shoulder. And now, as he cupped his hand towards her breast. And now, as he tousled her dark brown hair. *And now.*

Well, she said, wiping her mouth, that will ward off today's mortality blues.

Benji kissed her on the forehead. It was a Sunday. It was a good birthday, so far. Mortality blues, though? He disentangled himself from the sheets and stumbled to the bathroom to shower. There, he paused to assess himself in the bathroom mirror.

Behold: forty-four. His scruffy, curly-ish hair, once a dirty blond, was decisively turning salt-and-pepper. His grey eyes, his *orbs into the soul* – this is what Jen had called them last night, after quite a bit of wine, in a tone that he wasn't sure was serious, but why wouldn't she be serious? Anyway. He observed how his eyes were set in increasingly papery creases of skin. But as for the rest of him, he was in the best shape of his life. His mole-inflected belly was trim. His muscles lithe. He flexed his biceps in the mirror. Clenched his teeth into a hulky grimace. Yes.

He climbed into the shower that was, as all New York living dimensions seemed to be, borderline claustrophobic. Showering felt like spelunking, but he was only allowed to say that once. It's only funny once, Jen had told him, and the second time you just sound like you're not from New York. But I'm not from New York, Benji had protested. Nonetheless, he didn't say it again, opting just to think it each time he slid his body into the tiny vertical space. It was such a good word. *Spelunk.* He struggled to find the space to bend to lather his feet. Claustrophobic like that. *Spelunk.*

When he returned to bed, tossing the towel around his waist onto the floor, Jen was listening to the Goldberg Variations. He snuggled in with her.

Glenn Gould was Canadian, he commented, twirling a lock of her hair around his finger.

This isn't Gould, she replied tartly. Can't you tell from the phrasing? It's Víkingur Ólafsson. The *Icelandic* Glenn Gould.

Oh, he said.

—

An hour or so later, having dressed and brunched and wandering the streets of the city, the thought crossed his mind that, maybe, Benji didn't really know Jen that well. The realization was a burrowing thing. Did she even like him? He held her cashmere-gloved-hand carefully in his bare fingers. She was dressed for winter. A beret. A thick wool winter coat. A soft scarf. He wore a wool button-up shirt and didn't quite get the fuss. It was six degrees in Celsius, something else undramatic in Fahrenheit. Not cold. Even if he were underdressed, he was too distracted to feel a chill – everything here was a flurry. Bagels pressed up against fogging glass. Skyscrapers abutting sidewalks. Crowds pressed up against crowds.

This was the third time Benji had come to stay with Jen, and nothing was familiar yet.

She led him through the clotted maze of concrete to the outside of MOMA. She loved art. They joined a long line of fashionably dressed people. This was something else he had noticed about this city. The latent, layperson chic. There was a tastefulness, an attention to aesthetics, that manifested on the individual level here. It had intention. Everyone just looked so cool. When their turn came to security, however, Jen had to dump out her water bottle and throw out the energy bars in her purse. I had, she said blushingly, forgot about those.

Seven months earlier, they had met at a springtime half-marathon in Toronto. They were both runners. They had that in common, Benji reminded himself. She had a cousin up in Canada and had wanted to try to PB in the distance. (She did, by three minutes.) He had just won a world record. They bonded.

Oh yeah, because Benji was kind of a big deal. He had just broken the world record for the most T-shirts worn while running a half-marathon.

He had been stripping himself of T-shirts when she came over to talk. There had been almost one hundred. He peeled them off, ecstatically, in threes or fours. A big, sweaty pile on the pavement. It was a conversation starter.

It was, she had joked, all the striptease she needed to fall for him.

At MOMA, they filtered through the foyer, the crowd diffusing into the gallery halls. He followed Jen's confidence to the elevators, to the fifth floor. Western art from the 1880s to 1940s.

What a revelation. Never in his life had he seen so many Picassos. Some were bigger than he imagined – *Les Demoiselles d'Avignon,* huge. Some smaller, like *Bathers in the Forest.* They hid in unexpected places. Or Van Gogh. *Starry Night*! Just over there! Definitely in the category of smaller than expected. People gathered around it, smiling convincingly for selfies. It was a real crowd, with most people's backs to the art and their faces pointed towards their phones. He wormed his way towards the painting itself, photobombing who knows how many self-portraits, to observe its brushstrokes up close. Somehow, unsettlingly, he related the whole experience to drinking coffee at Starbucks.

Obviously, he wasn't exactly huge into art, but look, things kept capturing his attention. Like a Charlie Chaplin film projected against one of the white walls. Benji watched him being swallowed and eventually regurgitated by glistening machinery. *Modern Times,* he read on the wall beside the projection. He snickered as Chaplin, snaking flexibly through the giant cogs (what a small man he was!), paused to tighten some bolts. Then the machinery reversed course, and he slid backwards through the cog again. The film excerpt restarted. Benji watched it once more, laughing at the same spot for a second time.

As he wandered through a roomful of wire sculptures and ready-mades, Benji thought about his first days with Jen. After the race, jubilant, they had bonded over beer-garden beer. A series of commonalities emerged that progressively took on the drunken gleam of synchronicity. Both were fourteen when their mothers died, hers of cancer and his by suicide, deaths which summarized respectively unhappy illnesses. Their favourite movie was *The Royal Tenenbaums*. Neither had ever been to Paris, but both wanted to go. Their favourite sneakers were the Hoka Machs.

Those memories, now, were fused dolefully with his world record. He called it that, but technically it was untrue. Rather, it was a gloating tragedy. (Depending on his mood, he sometimes also called it that.) That day, he had finished the twenty-one kilometres in under three hours, which is all he needed to do for Guinness to accept his feat. Knowing it would take twelve weeks for ratification, he submitted the results the next morning. Expedited processing was a choice but involved an extra charge he couldn't justify to himself. He trusted that it would work out. In that processing period, however, someone else wrangled his way into one hundred and eleven shirts, ran a half-marathon, and, lacking the same monetary qualms as Benji, paid the eight hundred dollars to have the results ratified immediately.

By the time Guinness got around to considering his feat, it had already been surpassed. It was as if his record had never existed. On paper, it hadn't.

In the world of material facts, facts that stood solidly apart from arbitrary human recognition, unselfish and real (*real*, goddamnit!), however, it did.

Also, in his heart. It existed in his heart.

Nonetheless, this was a tough development. Soon enough, it was winter. The sun was always set. Seasonal depression settled into his bones. He focussed on being a good parent. Early-morning hockey practice, Tim Hortons coffees. Indoor birthday parties in industrial areas of town, where the ground was made of trampolines. How his children emerged, exhausted, stumbling on solid ground, mouths stained with candy, and he buckled them one by one into the cold car seats in his Honda Odyssey. It was, he liked to remind himself, the safest minivan on the market. Every time he thought this, he felt a pang in which he momentarily felt foreign to himself. *Who had he become?* But those thoughts, through repetition, began to stack together in this mind and, gaining substance like that, he started to realize: this. This was who he was. Back on black-ice roads, through the bluster, snow scurrying horizontally through the shaft of low beams in the wind, to the cream-coloured carpeted living room, cartoons, and a bath before bed. One week on, one week off.

On his birthday, Benji had observed how forty-four was a number hard to appreciate. It had some symmetry, but apart from that, it was a dull clang. In between here and there. Nothing fancy.

Back home, his father was watching the children. In the precise division of parenting time Benji had with his children's mother, this week was his. Occasionally, his phone dinged with photos that his father thoughtfully (and, frankly, somewhat unexpectedly; the man had only just bought a cell phone last year) sent. Hockey practice. The three rolling leafy wet snow into tiny globes and balancing them atop each other. The three watching movies in the living room.

Benji responded with generous strings of emojis. He wasn't sure what else to say. That life was intangible. Parenting was a physical relationship, the crush of soft flesh and obligation. The ghostly flash cellphone photography only highlighted absence.

At the gallery, he continued to wander, increasingly aware that he hadn't seen Jen for quite some time. Long enough that he was wondering if he should start to worry. In front of a bust of a woman, ants scurrying over her face, a baguette balanced on her head, he fumbled for his phone. Turning a corner, trying to decide if he was being silly in thinking to call, he found himself in front of Monet's *Water Lilies*. It was a whole room. The painting arced around the walls. It was like nothing else. The blues and purples and white reverberated inside of him. You could just stand there and absorb it. And there, magically, was Jen.

Hey, he whispered, nudging her arm. I've been looking for you.

Just think, she murmured, her eyes wet, he was going *blind* as he painted these.

Together, they explored on. The gallery started to seem endless. Jen stopped in front of a small bronze-like figure of a woman. The woman looked upwards with vacant bronze-sculpture eyes, her tresses of hair echoed by folds of fabric wrapped around her. Her two breasts were exposed, or one breast, the one with a slightly shinier tip, resembling a large areola, was. On the other side, her breast was flat like a penny, lopped off. This is Saint Agatha, Jen explained, the patron saint of mastectomies. According to Catholic faith, Agatha of Sicily was tortured for her Christian fate, after a governor of the Roman Empire tried to coerce sexual favours. She was a virgin. The governor was oppressing the Christian minority. Agatha, being the sort of woman of whom saints are made, refused on both principles. Cue the torture. After her breasts were removed with hot pincers, her chest allegedly healed, but she died days later when they rolled her over hot coals.

The saint was indirectly cast in a high-copper alloy and shows traces of a previous black lacquer, read Benji aloud. *Both breasts seem to have been prostheses, cast separately and soldered into place; only the right one remains. This gruesome detail reflects the morbid seventeenth-century interest in the lives and deaths of early Christian martyrs.* Well, then, he commented.

The small thing seemed misplaced, but the rest of the exhibit was outré feminist art, so maybe it made sense. A commentary. Jen peered closely at the back of Agatha's head and pointed. Look at that, she said.

Benji looked. There was a small hole in the back of Agatha's head for a halo.

When their eyes grew tired, they stopped at the coffee shop in the gallery, where, to a Canadian, everything felt very expensive. Benji nonetheless paid.

The coffee arrived in yellow Pantone mugs. Yellow 012.

Look, Jen said seriously. I need to tell you something.

Benji's stomach plummeted. His mind became a rippling panic. What was happening? Was she going to break up with him? On his birthday?

Okay, he said evenly.

Outside, the sky shuddered with a sudden dusk. The interior lighting edged up. Benji's hand damply grasped at his yellow coffee mug.

She confessed. After his last visit, she had decided to go through with the testing – what testing, Benji wondered – the testing for genetic proclivity to breast cancer. Remember? Her mom had *died* of breast cancer. The conversation was oblique, a sort of glossy confusion that didn't make much more sense afterwards to Benji, either. She was planning on cutting off her breasts. Prophylactic mastectomy. The surgery had already been scheduled, for a few months from now. She was scared but knew it was the right decision.

Just like Saint Agatha, I guess, he half-wheezed, distractedly. His mind had drifted with an immediate and alarming melancholy to her nipples.

Well, that reminded me that I hadn't told you yet.

That night, before dinner, Benji got dressed to go for a run. But as he was tying up his shoes, his dad FaceTimed and had the kids sing to him. Children are absurdism, especially in song. After they tried to have a conversation, man versus the chorus, but his middle child soon grabbed the phone off the table. He enthused about his Very Exciting Day, involving a neighbour coming to the door with a black cat that was not their black cat. As he rambled, he held the phone angled towards his soft, bluish chin. Scissor was inside the *whole time,* he gushed, swinging the phone around so enthusiastically that Benji had to turn away from his screen. (Look, Scissor! Dad is here!) Dad, the child insisted, ever astute to wandering attention, *Dad!* I want you to know. There are *two* black cats on our street! Dad! Say hi to Scissor!

Benji greeted the cat. He began to disentangle himself the conversation, a process of words and coaxing that felt almost corporeal, wondering the while where his dad was anyway. I love you, he cooed, over and over. Daddy will see you soon.

When he finally got out the door, the winter silence felt jagged. Central Park. The place wasn't real to him yet. It was a movie reference or a Zwift topography. Though he was not technically in the training cycle for his next world record attempt, he, out of habit, had put on all the running clothing he brought. He had brought a lot. The way that his arms became slightly numb had become something of a solace. His breathing felt reassuringly compressed against the layers of fabric.

He queued up the day's news podcasts. The city glistened with night and cold humidity. His nearly-worn-out Hokas slapped the pavement softly. As he listened, his arms becoming desensitized, his breathing becoming a little deeper, a bit restricted, he noticed something was happening. The words he was hearing, he realized, revealed themselves as colours.

Like "Giorgia Meloni." That was a cantaloupe-coloured name. "Bill Clinton," a slate grey. ("Hilary Clinton" was a brighter, bluer, shade of grey.) "Benjamin Netanyahu," a dark brown.

"Antonio Guterres," maroon. "Trump," navy blue. *But let's turn to today's world events,* cooed the podcast voice emanating from his earbuds. Benji couldn't fathom events or narrative. The colour of language swirled around him too compellingly. He stalled at each small marvel. Words were enough.

Suddenly, politics was nothing but white noise. Those world events just plotted unhappy themes. So historically unchanging they were, in fact, biblical: drought, wildfires, scourge, war. Maybe the Bible didn't have that much to say about the rise of fascism. "Fascism" was a marbly white word. The colour of a Roman bust. He had downloaded so many podcasts. Deutche Welle's *The World in Progress. The World* from PRX. CBC's *Your World Tonight,* and on the weekend, *The World this Weekend.*

So many podcasts, because he ran all the time. But now, he had this world of words. The kilometres buzzed along. He had the jarring feeling, even in the dark, of running through a video game. The turns and foliage were exactly like Zwift. He felt the slipperiness of déjà vu envelop him. And still, the white noise of world events in his ears. "Hamas." A brownish sort of pink.

It was a world of words.

"World," which occupied his throat in a weirder way the more he said it, was a blue-green. A weird word, *world.* The green had a hint of yellow in it, though, like the colour of the Sahara in a satellite image.

The word "word" itself was a bricky red, which also made sense.

His watch beeped another kilometre. He roused himself to look at the split. Five minutes, fifteen seconds. He was awash in sweat, cocooned in a fudgy humidity. His fingers were numb with cold. Time to turn around. Time to tell Jen about what was happening.

—

Well, Jen was unimpressed. You think "Giorgia Meloni" is cantaloupe-coloured, she observed dryly, because "Meloni" sounds like "melon."

She was finishing dinner, stirring a languid white sauce with mushrooms that glistened with butter and cream. Pasta – she had made it by hand – boiled tempestuously in a steaming pot. Despite the warm glow of the stove light, Benji had a thought: "Jen" was sea-urchin black. A spikey name.

But she poured him wine in a shattering sort of crystal or glass that was unfathomably, unownably fragile to anyone with children, and it was his birthday, and dinner was delicious, the pasta receiving a final flourish of freshly grated truffle, something he had heard of but never before experienced, and it was wonderful, as was everything that came later.

—

When the time came for the operation, months later, Benji was unable to take the time off work to fly to New York. He had used his vacation days before he knew. The kids had brought home viruses. He just couldn't leave. The first days were awful, for him far differently than for her. She sent him photos of herself post-op, thumbs up in her hospital bed.

The compressive bra covering her chest benignly resembled a sports bra. With the padding inside, she didn't look much different.

When she posted about it online, impossibly upbeat, that same thumbs-up pic post-surgery, he felt ashamed for his absence. He went for a run, another winter run. He layered on twenty-seven T-shirts.

Outside, he settled into the rhythm of breathing, stiff sneakers pattering against the cold snow. Soon, he felt that shimmering of words, though he was not listening to anything at all, just the sound of his breathing. A gentle percolating of thought. Warm sweat-soaked layers sweltered around him, but as he continued to run, the layers cooled and started to freeze.

He thought about flowers. What type he should buy her if he were to buy her a bouquet. Roses? He pondered floral semantics. It was her job. Roses were too obvious. *Flowers.* It was a miraculous word, actually, a shimmering non-colour of a word. He got lost in thought of it, a snowflake-like wind catching his face, and then he pushed his thoughts outwards again, pushed himself forward.

And, at a certain point, arbitrary like a revelation, he reversed course and started home.

Notes

Cantaloupe! is a rules-based piece of fiction. One of the constraints involved a bad joke from a joke-a-day calendar that someone gave my son, one of those ones that peels off a sheet of paper times three-hundred-and-sixty-five and generally lands on the floor. Not all the jokes are funny. You may not be surprised.

The intertitles in "The Two Lolas" are from *Macbeth*.

I'm no expert in drag kings so, for "A Guy Named Guy," I relied heavily on a few exceptional individuals practicing this very cool art form. The character of Guy was inspired by Albertan drag king Duke Carson, featured in CBC's *Canada's a Drag,* and the spectacular David Bowie alter-ego of a longtime mom pal, Moses Motors. The emcee was inspired by Murray Hill, whose YouTube videos are very funny. Those are his jokes, go check him out. All drag is great, but I'm a drag king girlie.

The phrase "Puns are pins on the map tracing the path from word to world" is from a *Paris Review* blog post by James Geary entitled "In Defense of Puns."

"Reasonable limits demonstrably justified in a free and democratic society" is from section 1 of *Canadian Charter of Rights and Freedoms,* Part 1 of the *Constitution Act,* 1982, being Schedule B to the *Canada Act 1982* (UK), 1982, c 11.

In "Oh Beautiful World!", "Now dark, now glittering, now reflecting gloom, now lending splendour" is from Percy

Bysshe Shelley's "Mont Blanc: Lines Written in the Vale of Chamouni," although with slightly differing punctuation. "God was alive, magic was afoot," is from Leonard Cohen's *Beautiful Losers*. Finally, Sarah Lucas's "Self-Portrait with Fried Egg" might be watching from the corner.

The statuette of Saint Agatha that I describe in "Modern Times" as living inside of MOMA in fact is a holding of the Met, a bronze standing 13.7 centimetres tall and dating from seventeenth-century Italy. Commentary in the story is derived from support materials on the Met website related to the piece.

Acknowledgments

I'm so grateful to Freehand for letting *Cantaloupe!* join its catalogue. My editors, Naomi and Kelsey, are an A-team. Naomi, what a great editor, reader, and queller of pre-publication nerves you are! Everything you edit or write is top-notch, so I hope that *Cantaloupe!* is no exception to your bookshelf of formidable literary judgment. I'm glad you found me in the slush pile! Kelsey, thank you for your excellent guidance, support and supplementary editing. And Natalie nailed it on the cover. Basically an astonishing feat of psychic transference. You are all amazing.

I test drove some of these stories with various first readers, including Kevin Spencer and Beth Ed. Thanks, pals! (You thought it was a thankless task, but I'm thanking you *right now*!) Also, appreciation to the ever-generous Greg Ioannou, who used an early version of the manuscript as an editing test for incoming staff at his editing company. Those nascent editors really had their red pens out! I'm glad that I could tweak the nuance of my exploration into the morality of living in a petro-state following in light of their commentary. Peter Midgley kindly gave feedback about the content related to South Africa and depictions of linguistic difference.

Earlier versions of "Miette is for Optimists" and "A Guy Named Guy" ran in *Prairie Fire* and *Plentitude*, respectively.

Other deep gratitudes: To Julie at Magpie Books for her aesthetic suggestions and for all the support Magpie gives me and other local writers! Independent bookstores are the best!

To my neighbours, Terri and Eddy, for being graciously on-call for my need for literary conversations.

Outside of words, I'm grateful for my running buddies and cycling buddies – particularly Dana, Larissa, Amanda, and Taylor – for tying my feet to the ground. The rambling, point-free conversations that evolve through endurance sport are the glorious anti-narratives to these stories. The heavily metaphorical mulch to the cantaloupe vines.

To the other parents I met through the once-small humans in my life, whose tacit solidarity for my off-kilter explorations of parenting, I hope, continue into their print manifestations. Many of these stories arose from feeling so at odds with my lot as a younger single parent, a psychic state that was abundantly obvious to those around me at the time. Love to you all.

To all my bad jobs for giving me the lead for literary alchemy and, occasionally, the time to type.

To Edmonton, *amiskwaciy-wâskahikan*, for being a persistently fantastic place to live, for all its under-sung arts and artists, for its stupendous river valley, and for being the template for these stories and all my stories.

Finally, for my family (parents, sisters, children, cats), and Robin for the debates, the road trips, certain company for whatever tickets I bought to plays/movies/openings on a whim, and generally for encouraging me just enough to then be tasked with enduring me. An h in the heart for you.

M.Jay Smith is an Edmonton/amiskwaciwâskahikan writer. She is the author of *the eclipse: poems after antonioni* (iguana) and poetry chapbook *the lucky incantation* (anstruther). Her nonfiction has appeared nationally and internationally, in places such as *Hazlitt, The Walrus, 18 Bridges, Los Angeles Times* and most Canadian newspapers. In school, she studied experimental poetry, aesthetic theory, and, later, law. She likes running, cycling, and telling jokes.